The Shakra

By, LeAnn Mathis

Other Books By LeAnn Mathis

<u>Monster Nights</u> - What happens when Monsters visit your town.

<u>"Little Red": An Autobiography</u> - Those fairytales were somebody's life. Mine!

Coming Soon

<u>Leo Leroy</u> - Something is horribly wrong with the school lunches and it is up to fifth grader Leo Leroy to find out the who, why, and what...and stop them.

Copyright 2014 By Hearth Publications
All rights reserved
Email HearthPublications@gmail.com
for rights and permissions or to contact the author

Table of Contents

Diviner....1
Goodbye....13
Captured....25
Attack....37
Unexpected Answers....45
Inspiration....61
King Cedric....69
Escape....79
Dragons....93
A Second Encounter....107
Reunion....121
Changes....141
Secret Passage....155
Breaking Up is Hard to Do....159
Transformation....169
Navestrung....179
Heart of the Mountain....193
The King's Secret....205
On Angel Wings....217
Land of the Starlings....225
The Last Reunion....239

Diviner

A gentle knock caught Saphira's attention. She looked away from the full length mirror her mother had let her borrow for the occasion and glanced at the door. Maria entered carrying a small bouquet of morning glories. She handed them to Saphira with a curtsey. "From your father, miss."

Saphira took a deep inhale of their soft perfume before reading the note that came with it. "For my own blossoming flower."

Saphira smiled and then handed the bouquet to Maria. "Could you add a few of these to my hair?"

"Of course." Maria pulled out three dark-blue buds and quickly pinned them to the sides of the bun. After examining the results, she pushed the bottom flower in more securely and declared it perfect.

Saphira asked Maria to bring the candlestick closer as she turned in front of the mirror, admiring herself from various angles. She reached her hand up and gingerly touched the silky petals that brought out the deep-blue of her own eyes and offset her blonde hair beautifully. Everything but a few curls had been swept into a high bun, but the candlelight magnified those locks so it looked like her dress was covered in golden prisms.

"I knew you would love them," a deep voice said from across the room. Saphira turned and smiled. Her father's coat and knee-breeches looked dyed to match the flowers he had delivered.

"I do. How did you find them at this time of year?"

He winked. "That's my secret." He looked behind him into the hallway and said, "Your mother *was* right behind me. Ah, here she is." He opened the door a little wider, and her mother rustled into the room. She wore her favorite dress, a pink satin gown under a laced black overlay. A drop pearl earring hung from one ear, and she was attaching its match to the other side as she entered. A small drawstring purse swayed on her arm.

When she finished, she made a spinning motion with one hand. "Let me get a look at you."

Saphira obliged and slowly rotated for her mother. The simple lines of Saphira's white muslin dress lent an extra elegance to her already graceful figure.

Her mother put a hand over her heart. "You're a woman already." She blinked back tears as she turned to her husband and added, "It seems impossible, doesn't it?"

Saphira resisted the urge to roll her eyes. Her mother had been saying that a lot lately.

Maria excused herself as her parents came further into the room. Her mother reached into her purse and pulled out a small velvet bag. "Happy Birthday."

Saphira grabbed it, loosened the top, and turned it over. "What is it?" she asked as its contents rolled out into her hand.

Her mother grinned. "You tell us."

Saphira held it up between her fingers and the room flashed with light. She watched, entranced, as a faint glow settled around the perfectly round orb. It had creamy white tones that swirled together on the surface, giving it a sense of movement. Sudden recognition made Saphira gasp. "It's a diviner!"

Saphira's mother nodded her head. "We know you love those old myths, and when we saw this in the marketplace, we knew we had found the perfect replica. Langor used the real one to help him discover his destiny, and now it's up to you to discover yours."

Saphira cradled it to her chest. "Thank you. It's perfect."

"Put it somewhere safe and then come join us. Our guests will be arriving soon," her father said before escorting his wife downstairs.

Saphira nodded and turned to her dresser. Opening the top drawer, she made a small nest for her "diviner" out of her softest nightgown. She placed the orb in the middle, but as she prepared to close the drawer, the light caught it one last time. She could have sworn she saw the swirls move, but when she blinked, the illusion stopped. Shaking her head, she finished closing the drawer and went to join her parents.

Her dress rippled around her feet as she hurried over the freshly sanded floors. The servants lined the entrance, ready to take people's cloaks and hats as she took the place of honor at the foot of the grand staircase. She looked past her parents on the right to the ballroom. The angle kept her from seeing a lot, but she could already hear the musicians playing one of her favorite tunes, Hendel's Minuet. She caught her hands beginning to play along. She stilled them as the door opened to receive their first guests of the evening.

The next two hours passed in a repetition of greetings. She welcomed them in her rich, alto voice but kept an eye towards the entrance, eagerly examining each new face. It seemed like forever before the procession of people began to die down and Saphira was allowed to leave her position. Her throat had become dry from all the greetings she had extended, and she wanted something to soothe it. Saphira paused as she entered the ballroom. It was the largest room in the house, and tonight it was crowded.

People lined the edges of the walls where rich, colorful banners and floral wreaths framed their faces. Several couples were dancing in the middle of the room creating a constantly changing mosaic of color as they moved through the steps. The soft hum of conversations mixed gently with the band's music and covered Saphira's quiet sigh as she realized there would be no easy way to reach the refreshment tables opposite her.

Passing through the crowd, she smiled and waved but avoided talking whenever she could. She saw Elena, her best friend, dancing with a tall young man in the middle of the room. Her dark hair revealed a surprising amount of red, and Saphira wondered if Elena had chosen her dress's color just for the effect it had on her hair. Her partner was having a hard time keeping up with the conversation and kept stuttering. He was unusually shy and hesitant, and Saphira knew she would have fun teasing Elena about her latest conquest later.

As Saphira worked her way towards the tables, her dance card filled with the names of young men she couldn't avoid. She had nothing against them, but her feet ached just thinking about her card. The last man to approach her carried two glasses of punch with him. He was tall and lean with skin bronzed from the sun. Instead of asking her to dance, he pled for mercy.

"Ma'am, I need your help. I accidentally left the table with one too many glasses. I need to get rid of it soon, or else I'll look like a fool. If you could find it in your heart to take one of these, then I would be forever in your debt."

The odd phrasing of his request made Saphira really look at him for the first time. His dark brown hair framed twinkling eyes, and she wondered which side door he had managed to slip through. "Jack! What are you doing here?"

"Trying to save myself from embarrassment. Since you greeted everyone here, you were the most likely to accept my drink out of sheer necessity. I would never have had the courage to approach you otherwise. You have changed so much since I last saw you, I barely recognized you."

Saphira laughed and took a cup, her throat no longer sore. "You weren't gone *that* long."

"I was gone long enough," he countered. Something about the way he said it made Saphira blush. He was already scanning the sides of the walls, and she hoped he hadn't noticed her reaction. "Hmm, there don't seem to be a lot of places left for us to sit down. Your parents did know they didn't have to invite everybody from Hallenbreth. They're just *friends* with the local Lord." Jack cocked his head towards her parents who were talking to Elena's father and mother.

Saphira looked over at them and smiled. "They knew, but I wanted to make sure you got an invitation too."

Jack laughed, but his eyes continued to search the room. They finally rested on the patio doors that led to the veranda outside. "Perfect," he said. "Follow me."

As she walked through the doors, silence reached out to her, dampening the noise from the party. The crisp, night air filled her lungs and her spirit expanded to take advantage of the new-found space. Living at the edge of town had its benefits. The view extended past Saphira's lands and a few farms to the very edge of the forest, but her eyes automatically went up. She smiled at the clear, cloudless sky.

"There you go, a seat fit for a queen," Jack said, and Saphira had to look back down to see where Jack was pointing. A stone railing lined the edges of the terrace except where steps opened towards the main lawn and garden.

Her eyes widened as she said, "I can't sit there."

"Why not? It has plenty of space, and the breeze is a luxury no other available seat can offer."

"Yes, but it's a *railing*. It could ruin my dress."

Jack's mouth formed a silent, "Oh." After a few moments of further examination, he snapped his fingers and said, "I've got it." He removed his coat and placed it over the edge of the railing. "Problem solved."

"But what about your coat?"

"It's the price I'm willing to pay to not have to talk about the weather, the party, or the people at the party." Jack shuddered.

Saphira laughed and traced the cloth lightly with her fingers. It still held some of his body heat. "I suppose I can try it for a few minutes."

Jack helped lift her into place so she wouldn't crease her dress, and blood rushed to her cheeks when his warm hands touched her waist. She kept her head partially down, pretending to adjust her dress until her cheeks had cooled and her heart stopped beating so fast.

When she looked back up, Jack was swinging himself gracefully into place next to her. The movement reminded her of when they were children and used to climb trees together. She wondered if he kept in practice on the trail. The thought of him racing the other traders up a tree made her chuckle. She could already hear him taunting his nearest competitor. "Try not to breathe too heavily. Your breath can knock even *me* down in the morning; I'd hate to see what it might do to the tree."

"What are you laughing at?" Jack asked, interrupting her thoughts.

"Nothing. I was just thinking how kid-like you can be at times." Saphira leaned back and let her feet dangle.

"Is that a good thing, or a bad thing?"

Saphira looked at him from the corner of her eye and smiled. "It's a good thing."

"Then let's toast," he said as he grabbed his cup. "To the simple joys of life."

Saphira lifted her own glass and clinked glasses with him before taking a sip. The fruity blend slid down her throat and reminded her of summer. She would have to ask the cook to make this again another time. It was perfect. She took another sip and let the flavors work their way slowly around her tongue before swallowing.

"It's wonderful to be back home again." Jack sighed contentedly. "I feel as happy as Drayden after he drank Midax's enchanted wine."

Saphira turned her head towards Jack. "Drayden? Is he one of your new finds?"

Jack nodded. "He's very popular in Burbish stories. They even gave him his own constellation. He, Midax, and Elexa make up 90 percent of their myths."

"Elexa was there, too! I don't care what other people say. She must have been real. There are too many stories about her."

Jack's eyes twinkled. "I agree. I don't know how much is true and what has been exaggerated, but something happened. Although, few defend her existence as passionately as you."

Saphira waved her hand dismissively. "Someone has to. Now tell me what you heard."

"If you insist." Jack swung back off the railing and cleared his throat. Standing so that the light from the ballroom hit his face, he began his tale.

"The people were preparing for battle, but the war was not going well. Elexa looked around at her army. They were tired, and she didn't know how much longer they could last.

The elves were camped next to them, but even their added strength would not be enough to defeat the navestrungs. They never tired, never stopped.

"Elexa turned her back on their fires and left, searching for answers. It seemed hopeless. Every plan for defense, every offensive strategy led to the same awful conclusion. They would not survive. She walked until she could no longer hear the hum of knives being sharpened or the screams of nightmaring soldiers.

"In the quiet, she reached for her one weapon those monsters truly feared - a shakra. It alone had the power to kill them. The shakra was a gift from the starlings, forged to defeat the very elements that defined and created those demons. But the enemy was too numerous. She couldn't defeat them all.

"Frustrated, Elexa pounded a nearby tree with her shakra. Each word became a stroke as she called out, 'Why can't we stop them?' As the tree fell down, so did Elexa. Doubling over, she let her sobs overtake her.

"Elexa lay there until she felt the soft, soothing rhythm of wings beating air against her face. 'You're back.' She said quietly, in disbelief, not wanting to scare them. The starling's small, blue bodies were barely noticeable against the night sky. She pleaded gently, 'Is there anything you can do to help us?'

"'Yes,' they said softly in return, 'but it would require great sacrifice on your part. You could wield the shakra with enough power to stop your enemies, but you would change into something not quite human. You would never be able to return to your people.' Elexa suffered only the briefest hesitation before accepting their offer and leaving with them for their last journey into the sky.

"The next day, the navestrungs attacked. Her army looked around, wondering where their hero had gone. With no hope to win, they were about to retreat when the navestrungs suddenly stopped, screaming in terror and pain. Something was attacking them. The humans watched in amazement as the enemy quickly disbanded and ran to the mountains for safety. They and their allies were saved.

"Wanting to thank their protector, they searched but couldn't find who, or what, had rescued them. That evening, when they said their night prayers to the sky, a soldier noticed a new constellation. Hidden among the stars was a stance he recognized. He ran through the camp, showing everyone what he saw. Elexa was facing the mountain, poised for battle.

"Realizing what happened, they looked up in the sky and thanked her, vowing to carry her story with them wherever they went. They felt more than heard her response: 'Go in peace. I shall always be here, watching over and protecting you.'"

"Wow, that was amazing," Saphira breathed, not wanting to break the quiet of the moment. Jack lowered the arm he had extended while relaying Elexa's final speech and rejoined her. No matter how many times Saphira heard the story, she never got over her awe for Elexa. Would she have been so quick to sacrifice herself for her people? She didn't know. "Elexa definitely earned her right to be remembered among the stars."

Jack nodded. "Yes, she did. As far as I know, Drayden's the only one who was able to sneak up there uninvited."

"What? How did he do that?"

"It was an accident. He was trying to get away from a very angry minotaur and wasn't looking when he ran looking right into the sky." Jack looked up and twisted his head until he was staring in the southern right portion of the sky. "You can see him right there." Jack traced the outline with his fingers.

"Do you see that bright star just above the tree line? That's his foot. If you follow that line of stars all the way up, you will see the cluster of stars that make up his face. He's still running away."

Saphira's laughter attracted the notice of a previously ignored suitor. "There you are," he said. Frowning at Jack, he informed Saphira that she had promised him a quadrille and the dance was forming now. She hoped he was wrong, but when she checked her dance card, she saw his name followed by a long list of other gentlemen's names. She wished she had allowed herself one more song before accepting partners, but it was too late now. She inwardly sighed. She would not be back.

She looked over at Jack and knew he had seen her list. "It looks like the rest of your evening is full," he said. "We will have to finish our conversation later. Perhaps I could visit you tomorrow after the market closes?"

Saphira's heart skipped a beat. Had she heard right? He had never tried to visit just her before. She could hear Elena's voice in her head say, *If a boy visits you, alone, then it means something.* She knew what that something was, but she tried to respond as casually as she could. "That would be fine. I look forward to seeing you tomorrow."

Jack held her hand as she slid off the railing. He squeezed it before letting go. "Until tomorrow," Jack said, bowing out of the way. She forced herself to smile as she took her partner's hand and accompanied him back into the warm, stuffy ballroom.

Several hours later, she finally collapsed on her own bed. After Maria had helped her get changed, she couldn't resist pulling out the diviner one more time. She placed it on her pillow next to her and let the moonlight light up its surface. The little beams that reflected back off its surface made it look like it was filled with stars.

"My destiny is going to be wonderful, isn't it?" Saphira said to no one in particular.

As she fell asleep, she dreamt the stars rearranged themselves into Elexa's constellation.

Goodbye

Saphira woke up to the sun streaming on her face. She blinked and a slow smile spread across her face as she thought about the previous night's activities. The evening couldn't have gone better. All her friends had come, even Jack, and…Wait! The sun was too bright. She jumped out of bed and ran towards the window. It couldn't be afternoon already. The marketplace closed early today, and if his day ended before hers began, she would never hear the end of it.

After calling for Maria, she ran to her dresser and picked out her outfit. She crammed in slices of buttered toast and jam between clothing layers and could barely keep from jumping with excitement. While her parents thought she was still too young to decide who she wanted to marry, no one else could compare. Every moment in his presence seemed to strengthen her attachment to his teasing, knowledgeable, entertaining person. There were times that she thought he might feel the same way towards her, but until last night, she hadn't been sure. Of course, she had always been too young - before.

She glanced out the window after she was dressed and saw him heading up the street. She ran to the receiving room and flung herself on the couch. Then she jumped back up, grabbed her embroidery bag from the corner and rushed back to her seat. She normally sat in the green chair closest to the window when she sewed, but the flowered brocade on the couch set her skin off better and had enough room for another person to sit by her. She smoothed her dress down between gasps of breath.

Maria had entered the room while Saphira was bustling about and waited until she was settled, before walking over to the Saphira's couch. Saphira quickly shook her head, silently begging "no" with her eyes. Maria paused and eyed her narrowly, but then continued around the couch to the window chair. Saphira mouthed out, "Thank you," before grabbing her hoop and threads out of the bag. She gave a sigh of relief when she found a half-finished project already secured inside the hoop. She had just made her first stitch of the day when the butler opened the door and announced, "Jack Kinyard."

Jack strolled in shortly afterwards, and the breath Saphira had been trying so hard to control stopped. Somehow the wind-blown hair that he had obviously tried (and failed) to smooth down was more alluring than his carefully crafted hair of the night before. As she gazed, she almost said, "I love you," but she was able to change it to a cough after the "I."

"Would you like some water?" Jack asked, but she shook her head and motioned for him to sit. Jack sat down next to her and said, "I must admit I'm a little surprised. I didn't think you'd be up so early after last night's ball. I half expected you to still be sleeping."

Saphira smiled. "As you can see, you were quite wrong. While I was waiting, I was able to get a little more work done on a sampler I've been making." She lifted it up so he could see it better. Ignoring Maria's snort, she continued, "So, how was the market today?"

Jack told her about his supplies and how well they sold, and then he began telling her more about where they came from, and how they acquired them. She would have been more interested, but she kept waiting for when he would talk about his real reason for coming over. When Maria left to fetch some refreshments, Saphira's heart began beating erratically. First it pounded against her chest, and then it began skipping beats. It was several minutes after Maria returned with the cucumber sandwiches for her heart rate to return to normal.

Jack said several nice things to her but never anything *in particular.* When he began telling her about the trick Drayden pulled with his food, she started screaming inside. She wanted to talk about love, not pie.

Apparently, he felt differently. If only Elena had never made her stupid comment about visiting boys, then she might have been easier in his company and actually enjoyed the stories.

When he promised to visit her the next day, she vowed not to get her hopes up. Elena would call it a sign that he was interested, but she was wrong about today, and tomorrow wouldn't be any different.

Or so she thought, but his hand kept touching hers. It couldn't be a coincidence. She was so distracted by what his hands were doing she couldn't remember what they talked about. She could only recall their calloused warmth against her skin.

There began to be lulls in the conversation, and Saphira wondered what he was not saying. Were they the same things that occupied her mind? When he kissed her hand goodbye, she could have sworn his hold lingered.

By the end of the week, whenever Maria stepped out for a quick second, their fingers intertwined around each others. Maria was fetching some paper for Saphira when her father came in. Their hands unlinked as her father scanned the room. He walked over to the chair he had occupied last night and picked it up. He then sat down and began to read. He didn't say anything, and Saphira began to relax, but she did note that he didn't leave again until Jack had ended his visit.

On subsequent visits, she noticed that Jack reached for her hand a lot less. Had she said something to make Jack lose interest? Had her father said something? Had he never really been interested? She realized that for all their handholding, he hadn't confirmed a future with the two of them together. Maybe he just remembered that it wasn't the custom to hold hands with everyone in Hallenbreth. She blushed as she thought about the moment he realized what his actions might have meant to her. And what they meant about her feelings for him. But at least he didn't stop coming.

A week later, Elena invited them to a garden party. Her grounds were famous for their elaborate shrubbery maze, but there was also a large open section of lawn where she promised croquet and other games would be set up. Saphira hoped she might get the chance to ask him how he felt about her during that time. If the news was bad, then the croquet game would give her an excuse for keeping her head down. She didn't want him to know how much he could hurt her.

They arrived early, and Elena directed them towards their seats by the rose bushes. Jack was pulling out a chair for Saphira when a voice boomed towards them, "Well, well, well. If it isn't Jack and Saphira. How are you two doing?"

They looked over and saw a well-dressed couple coming towards them. "Casper, Angela, it's wonderful to see you again," Jack replied as he shook one of Casper's big beefy hands. Even though they were the same height, Casper filled up twice the space Jack did. He would be intimidating if it weren't for the smile he always wore. "How's your textile business doing?"

"You should know. You sell most of the goods our father produces," Angela responded with a half-smile. She then coughed gently, and Casper pulled her chair out for her.

Once she was seated, Casper took his place by Jack. "Elena said that you two would be our table partners. I'm so glad. There is always a tendency towards boredom at these things unless people at your table can say something interesting. I trust I won't run into that problem here."

Saphira shook her head and looked at Jack with pride. "Not here. Jack is filled with more stories then I can count."

"Then we will have to make sure he shares them." Casper nudged his sister in the arm. "What do you think

Angela? What method should we use to entice him to speak: torture, or bribery?"

Angela smoothed the sleeve down where her brother touched her before looking at Jack. "Torture. It's more efficient."

"Then torture it is." Casper pointed his finger at Jack. "Did you hear that? If you don't tell us a story, then we'll tell you in excruciating detail how cloth is produced: from cotton seeds, to pesticides, to the final weave of the fabric."

Jack laughed and threw his hands up. "You win. I'd rather do anything than learn about plant poison at a picnic. What would you like to hear?"

"Your best travel stories. What's life like outside Hallenbreth? If I ever get a chance to leave, where should I go? What should I try?"

"That all depends on how strong your stomach is and how much adventure you can handle." Jack paused while a servant distributed everyone's food. He looked down at his plate and picked up a small sandwich. He pointed to the orange filling and said, "This is almost the exact same coloring as a stew they make in Titus." Jack took a small bite; then a bigger bite. With his third bite, it was gone.

"That was delicious, but Titus's version is revolting. It's ninety percent snail, and they offer it as a 'delicacy' to their visitors. The local inns hold bets to see how many strangers will throw up after eating it. I was able to keep it down, much to the disappointment of my older colleagues, but I couldn't get rid of the aftertaste for days."

As the meal progressed Jack told them other stories of his adventures. Most of them were funny, revolving around the oddities of the people he had met on his travels. He had to stop talking several times so someone at the table could recover from trying to eat and laugh at the same time.

"I've had the wrong calling in life. I am now going to renounce the textile business and begin trading. I can't believe I've missed so much in my life," Casper said.

"Yes, but I should warn you that it is not always safe to travel to such exotic places. The land can turn against you, swallowing whole wagons in the sandpits by the southern oceans or the eastern swamps. Thieves and wild animals pounce on you the moment you let your guard down until you reach the southwest borders, where the gnomes beat them to it.

"The gnomes are violent creatures, but they can produce things that are just…incredible. There are no real words to describe the feelings and wonder that these pieces evoke. You've heard of the tiara of Middletore and the armor of Gonerall?" Everyone around the table nodded. Jack continued, "They made them. I once saw a miniature forest they made, and I kept waiting for the wind to stir the branches and the animals to move.

"Our artists have been trying to replicate their work for years but haven't come close. It has only been the last few years that the gnomes have allowed us to enter their lands to trade. Their mountains hold the purest veins in the world, and artists pay a fortune for it.

"But don't think you can steal their ore. They constantly roam their lands for intruders. If people get too close they are labeled trespassers and become enslaved in the mines. There has been a lot of tension along the border by people claiming the gnomes are taking people beyond their boundaries, but some of the borders are hard to distinguish, and nothing's been proven.

"One time, we were traveling south and went further than we intended, accidentally crossing into their borders. We had unhooked our horses so they could rest in the shade when one of our crew started shouting something about gnomes. He got on his horse and galloped away. As soon as the rest of us registered what he said, we were out of there, too."

"What did they look like? I've heard rumors, but not from anyone who has actually seen one," Angela said.

Everyone around the table leaned in a little closer.

"When I first saw them, they reminded me of us: two arms, two legs, but with eyes as big as a grown deer's. The resemblance disappeared completely, however, when they moved. They became bat-like nightmares as their ears swooped out to the sides, and they flew at us from every direction. Glints of light reflected off their armor, weapons, and teeth."

The girls shivered. "I guess the rumors were true. That must have been terrifying."

"It was. Fortunately, all our horses had reins or leading ropes on them so all we had to do was get on them and ride away. Charlemane, our accountant, did try to save our wagons, but he only had time to grab the money bag before the gnomes descended on him. They sliced half-way through his arm before he was able to get away.

"He was bleeding heavily and swaying in his seat by the time we reached the next town. Luckily, the local doctor was able to stitch his arm back together, and he only lost feeling in two of his fingers. All Charlemane would say about his foolhardy action was that he refused to see us totally ruined."

"Incredible," Angela murmured almost to herself.

"Your table looks much too serious," Elena interrupted them, and the mood shifted as she walked over to them. The other people had finished their meals and were already beginning to separate. "We're getting a game of Blind Man's Bluff started, and we could use some more players."

"That sounds like fun. Why don't we all go?" Casper looked around the group.

"I'm afraid we only have room for two more players," Elena said. "Since this is Jack's first time here, I'd like to send him to the maze and see if he can find his way back out before the next round begins. Since Saphira knows where we keep the maze ribbons, she can get him started if you and Angela want to play this round."

After everyone agreed, Elena whisked her two players away. Saphira was standing to leave as well when out of the corner of her eye she saw Elena look behind her and wink at Jack. Saphira gritted her teeth. When had they become so friendly? "I'll meet you at the entrance," she said curtly and stormed off.

As she pulled the ribbon from the gardener's cupboard, she chided herself. What if she hadn't seen what she thought she saw? She was overreacting. Elena would never try and take Jack away from her.

Her heart melted at his smile as she joined him at the slender pole that marked the beginning of the maze. As she positioned the spool around the pole she heard Jack say, "Do you know I really like your friend Elena?"

Saphira's hands lost their grip and the ribbon slid quietly to the bottom. She hadn't been imagining things! He was breaking up with her, and Elena was to blame. At least she'd be able to cry in semi-privacy. She didn't want to hear what came next, but she had to know. She held onto the pole for strength. "What do you like so much about her?"

Jack took the end of the ribbon and then grabbed Saphira's hand, gently leading her into the maze. "Because she very craftily arranged to have us slip away from the rest of the party."

Saphira could barely believe it. She had been such a fool. How could she have thought so poorly of her best friend? She leaned closer and wrapped her fingers around his as the maze's high walls soon shielded them from view.

"You know, I love this," Jack said. "Holding your hand is so comforting. I don't know why that is, but I'll miss it when I'm gone.'"

Saphira stepped back. "Gone? Is it already time for you to leave again?"

Jack turned and nodded. "We leave tomorrow. Our company has just been approved to trade with the gnomes. We put in the paper work years ago and never thought we'd be approved."

"But...but, they attacked you and hurt Charlemane. What's going to stop them from doing it again?"

"We'll be entering their land properly this time. They've never hurt the designated traders. This opportunity will allow me to buy a house and open a shop sooner than I'd dared to hope for. I'd be able to settle down and have a wife and family."

"You would give up traveling?" Saphira couldn't believe it.

"I'd have to. I have a hard enough time walking away from you as it is. If you married me, then I don't know how I could ever tear myself away."

Saphira put her free hand over her chest. Her heart was beating out of control. "Jack, are you asking what I think you are asking? I'm so happy. I don't know what to say."

Jack looked at the ground. "Don't say anything," he whispered. He turned away from her and gripped a branch. "I'm sorry, but I cannot ask you yet."

Saphira's hand dropped. "I don't understand."

"Your father objects. He says until I have a more stable career, he cannot entrust you to my care. I wish he felt differently. I hate the thought of all those men drooling after you and trying to steal your affections while I'm gone. If they succeed, then I don't know if I could survive the rejection."

Saphira touched his shoulder, and he turned to look at her.

"You don't need to worry about them," she said, resting her hand against his cheek. "Absence makes the heart grow fonder."

"Or forgetful," Jack said, lowering his eyes.

"I could never forget you!"

Jacks gaze traveled back into her eyes, and his whole expression softened. He lifted her chin with his finger and kissed her, lovingly and tenderly. It expressed better than words how much he cared for her and would miss her when he was gone.

Bless Elena for thinking of the maze.

Captured

The sky was rosy pink when Saphira met Jack at the gates. Jack was tossing the last few bags into the wagon when he saw them. Maria stood a few inches behind Saphira and was stifling a yawn, but Saphira's face held a false smile that Jack instantly recognized. He walked over to where they had paused to watch him. Maria fell back a little ways and began to study her shoes.

Jack stroked the side of Saphira's cheek. "There's no need to look so sad. After we leave, there will still be time to join your friends at Condor's Chapel. I heard they were going to make a picnic out of it."

"I can't imagine how you think I could possibly want to attend any parties when you can't be there with me. I woke up and realized that this is the last time I will see you for a really long time. I'll miss you so much."

"Not as much as I'll miss you, but you don't have to avoid *all* your friends while I'm gone…just the men. Besides, you'll need some stories to tell me when I get back. I'll be so thirsty to hear your voice that if you run out of things to talk about, I'll make you read inventory lists to me."

Saphira's half-laugh made Jack smile. "That's my girl. I knew you'd come around. Now go, enjoy yourself, and I'll be back before you know it."

A man near the wagon shouted towards him, "Are you two finished?"

"Yes," Jack shouted back. He then continued in a softer voice, "You'll hear from me soon. I promise." He kissed her on the cheek and went to join the others.

Saphira heard the companion call out, "Charlemane, you take Perkin with you on the first wagon, and Oscar, you take Benjamin. The rest of you, get on a horse and ride out."

The dust rose around them as they set out. Just before they turned the corner Jack turned and waved at Saphira. She raised her hand in recognition but couldn't bring herself to wave back. Blinking back tears, she wandered until she stood before the house of the one person who understood exactly whom she had just said goodbye to.

"He's gone," she said, collapsing into Elena's arms.

Elena patted her back as she said, "I know. I'm sorry. He had seen me the day before the party and asked for my help. He said there was something he wanted to tell you in private. I was sure I knew what that meant – until you left the maze. I was so mad, I cornered Jack about it later. How could he use me to break your heart? But he said it wasn't like that. He then told me everything."

"Everything?" Saphira's voice squeaked as she pulled back.

Elena looked at her friend's reddening cheeks. "Apparently not. What else happened in there?"

Saphira whispered everything about the almost proposal and the kiss. Elena shrieked and sighed at the appropriate moments. Saphira then told her about seeing him off. "I didn't think I'd be able to stay upright against the pain. I felt like my heart was ripped from my chest when he turned that last corner and left my sight. How will I survive until he comes back? It's never been this hard to say goodbye before."

"That's because he wasn't *yours* before, and he wasn't going to be gone for as long."

Saphira pulled out a handkerchief. "Thanks for reminding me."

Elena patted her arm. "Don't worry. I have the perfect distraction for you."

Saphira sniffed. "What?"

Elena leaned in conspiratorially. "Finding *my* love. Now that you've found your ideal partner, I'm jealous. The way I figure it, if I have two people looking for him, then I'll find him twice as fast. Right?"

Saphira answered cautiously, "I guess so."

"Good. Now tell me what you think about Derek Killobaker." Saphira forgot her own pain for a moment and burst out laughing as she imagined portrait-perfect Elena with "Dirty" Killobaker.

Several hours later, Saphira was on her way home when she saw the Odds and Ends shop. It contents varied greatly during the year, and she entered it, hoping to find a fun little trinket to send Jack with his first letter. She found something even better. She held it to her chest and purchased it immediately.

Back in her room, she found a spot on her wall to hold her newest possession. The map contained all the known settlements in the kingdom. She found Hallenbreth first, just below the Elves' territory. She scanned her way south until she found the upside down Vs that marked the mountains the gnomes called home. When she calculated the distance, she almost cried. Hundreds of miles separated them.

Pulling back the tears, she drew a dot near Hallenbreth, and wrote the date. Whenever she got a note from Jack, she vowed to record where he was and when he sent it. Even though she couldn't be with him in person, she would travel with him on the map.

For several months she marked the towns he journeyed through, occasionally writing down notes about the things he had seen on his trip. Her map was getting full, but despite these visible signs that he still thought of her, they came too far apart to make her comfortable.

What if he changed his mind and didn't want to be with her when he came back? What if she changed *her* mind? No, impossible. They were destined to be together. Nothing could change that.

She imagined all the ways she would greet him when he returned. She pictured herself standing at the gates waiting for him. As soon as he lifted his weary eyes from the road, he would see her and immediately leave his caravan behind to race towards her. He would jump from his horse so he could sweep her up into a massive bone-crushing hug. She would smile up at him and tease him about his lack of faith. "How could you have ever doubted me?"

Then again, she could pretend not to know him at first and say, "But who are you good sir? I was waiting for my love, and you could not possibly be he. He is not nearly so tan."

If she wanted to be truly cruel, then she would make him seek her out. He would stand before her, holding her hand, begging for the return of her affections. She would look down at him and say haughtily, "Jack, I fear that after your prolonged absence, I cannot give you any more regard." He would look stricken and turn away from her before she would take pity on him, touch his arm, and say in a much warmer tone, "for you have my whole heart and have held it this entire time."

Looking at the map, Saphira traced her finger along the arc that marked the areas Jack had already traveled. She could see his trail curving west, towards the mountains, and she tried to guess where he'd write to her next and how it would be affected by the journey. Some of them were torn, others had gravy stains, and almost all of them had ink spatters or long pen lines from where he got jostled while writing. She picked up some of his more recent letters and opened one to read again.

Dearest,

I miss you, and I wish I could have known before I left what I know now. It seems all our haste was wasted. The tanning specialist we came to see is in Hurst visiting his daughter's family and won't be back for several days. The others won't trade his stuff without him. There is nothing we can do but wait. I hate being idle because I know that this is time that I could have been spending with you.

To make it worse, I heard something today that almost made me leave this behind and come running back. They have a legend about a beautiful maiden named Rhonda. She was as kind as she was lovely with long black hair that gathered in soft curls and eyes that sparkled more than the sun. Everyone who saw her couldn't think of anything else but her. Several people wanted to marry her, but her father refused them all.

One day, a very rich man saw her. He immediately went to ask her hand in marriage. The father was so blinded by the man's treasures, he didn't consider what kind of husband the man would be and agreed. When he introduced his daughter to the suitor, she was disgusted. He was old, ugly, and rude to anyone he wasn't trying to please.

That night she went into her garden and cried her sorrows to the moon. The moon heard her tears and resolved to save her. He jumped down from the sky and carried her back with him.

When her father went to look for her the next morning, she was nowhere to be found. He and her betrothed searched in vain for her. The suitor gave up after a few weeks, but the father continued to search for years. He wished there was some way he could make amends, but he didn't know where to start.

Seeing how sorry the father was, the moon carried Rhonda to her father's house for a visit. The father could barely contain his happiness, but after five minutes he was forced to recognize an awful truth. She returned the moon god's love and would not be staying.

The god, seeing the pain her departure would cause the father, arranged it so he would always be able to see her and how happy she was. When the father looked up into the sky the next night he was surprised to see his daughter smiling down on him.

I'm telling you this story as a warning not to enlist any god's help to avoid persistent suitors. They might take you away like they took Rhonda. After all, you are lovelier than she could have possibly been. (At least to me.)

    Missing my real Rhonda,
    Jack

She folded it and put it back in its envelope and reached for the next one. It was his most recent letter and had arrived five days ago. It was all about their preparations and how excited (and nervous) he was to trade with the gnomes. She flipped the seal over but didn't get a chance to read it before there was a knock at the door.

"Come in," Saphira said, and her parents entered the room.

"Are we interrupting anything?" her mother asked. She looked paler than usual.

"No, I was just reading. What can I help you with?"

"Nothing. We just…we had something we needed to tell you." Her mother glanced at the letters and the map behind Saphira but just as quickly looked away. She found a stool and sat by Saphira, taking one of her hands.

"What is it?"

Her mother stroked Saphira's hand while she searched for words. Finally she said, "Do you remember Dunkin? He watches the market for us in the south."

"Yes," Saphira said slowly.

"He just sent us some horrible, horrible news." Her mother stopped, unable to say what came next.

Her father placed his hand on his wife's shoulder. "Jack's trading group has been sent to the mines. We don't know what went wrong, but they won't be coming back."

"Impossible! Gnomes don't do that to trading parties. Jack *promised* me he'd be safe."

"He should have been. That's what makes this so awful. When Dunkin heard the news, he sent us a direct message. He knew we had known them."

"Known them!" Saphira drew back her hand. "You talk like they are already dead, but Jack and his men would never do anything wrong. The gnomes will realize their mistake and release them. They might already be freed."

Her mother shook her head. "They might be, but it has never happened before."

"No!" Saphira jumped up and stormed away from her parents. Jack...captured...now? It wasn't possible.

Her father started after her, but his wife held his arm and shook her head. "Give her time. She not ready to accept the truth, yet."

###

More than two months passed, and Saphira still hadn't heard from Jack or learned anything about his possible release. Even though she knew in her core that he was still alive, it didn't look like he was coming back anytime soon. She remembered what he had said about the gnomes at Elena's party the day before he left. She shuddered and thought of him being whipped and starved under their unfeeling eyes.

She went to her room and pulled out her diviner. It shimmered in the light cast from her window, and she remembered how she had planned to have it set into a tiara for her wedding day. She held it above her head and tried to picture the day as she had imagined it. The sun, sparkling through the church's clear glass windows. The diviner, catching that radiance and spreading it around her being until her whole essence glowed - from the flowers in her hands to the trailing ends of her flowing gown. She would regally pass by all her friends and family until she reached the end of the altar where Jack would wait, wearing a huge smile on his face that he would try, unsuccessfully, to remove whenever he remembered the solemnity of the occasion. He would take her hand those last few steps and together they'd turn and face the priest who joins them together at last.

But it wasn't working. When she looked down the aisle this time, she saw… nothing. All the glittering tiara illuminated was an ashen bride, empty benches, and a barren altar. She took the tiara out of her hair and held it in her hands, its brightness a mockery of her pain.

She blinked back tears and croaked, "How can I ever be happy again?"

She flung the diviner onto her bed and prepared to walk away when the light coming from the diviner shifted position. Saphira stopped. She bent over, and picked the stone back up. Pinpricks of light she hadn't noticed before jumped along the surface as she turned the orb around.

The sequence seemed vaguely familiar, and she traced her finger from one point to the next until she realized it was the constellation for the journey god, Tournus. She laughed in frustration. Tournus had travelled to the underworld to save his beloved, but Saphira would never be able to rescue *her* love, not from the gnomes. She couldn't even join him in his abyss.

She went over to the map, and placed a hand over the mines. She looked up and found Hallenbreth, staring at the distance between them. She tried to get Tournus's story out of her head. The gnomes were too far away; she would never make it. Unless… She moved her hand and used it to trace a road line connected to a nearby town. It travelled right to the gnome's kingdom.

Thoughts swirled in her head as her heart pumped loudly in her chest. She had visited that town before. She could find it on her own if she had to. Once there, all she would have to do is follow the road, and she would be reunited with Jack. Maybe she could even help the gnomes see reason, and they would release Jack. If they did, then they could return home, and…. She could finally see her wedding day happening again.

She ran to her closet and began pulling out her sturdiest clothes.

Attack

    The clock struck twice just as Saphira released her father's short sword from its pegs on the study wall. Her fingers instinctively spread apart, and she almost dropped it, but she grabbed it again before it hit the floor. She remained hunched over it for several breaths after the last chime's echo died away.

    She slowly straightened and listened carefully for signs of movement as she moved over to the couch where she had placed her bag. It held all the supplies she hoped she would need for her trip. She rummaged inside until she found a letter addressed to her parents. Pulling it out, she placed it on her father's desk and left. She knew nothing could convey her assurance that she was doing the right thing, but she had tried.

    The stables were her last stop. In the few days it had taken to gather her supplies, she had decided against her customary side saddle for a treeless one. It was designed for endurance and comfort, two things she would want, but it meant she would have to walk to the tree line. Her horse,

Penelope, wasn't used to the other riding style, and she didn't want her neighing this close to the house.

It was over an hour before Saphira's heart beat slowed down. She was well within the borders of the forest by then. She followed one of its meandering paths to a blackberry patch she and Elena had discovered last summer. She hoped the thorny stems would help protect her from wild animals. Its white flowers were just starting to bloom, and they added a pleasant scent to the night air. She tied Penelope's bridle to a low hanging tree branch near the thicket and started rummaging through her bag.

Relying mostly on touch, she pulled out the cloth objects and was able to distinguish a cloak, shirt, and a pair of pants. Putting the rest back in the bag, she changed into her new outfit. Covering the ground with her dress, she lay down, wrapping her thick cloak around her. She would finish the rest of her changes in the morning.

When she woke up, Saphira wondered why her bed felt so lumpy and hard. She groaned and rolled over, trying to go back to sleep, until she realized where she was. She hadn't thought about how uncomfortable sleeping on the ground was going to be. The excitement to rescue Jack lessened, but she was still determined to try. She gave herself a grim shake and began preparations for the final break from her old life.

She took out a comb and detangled her mass of hair until it fell down her shoulders in a neat line. Tugging on a section at a time, she sliced it off with the sword until it was only two inches from the bottom of her ears.

Her head felt light and foreign. She placed the sword carefully on the ground and glanced at the pile of hair. It looked dull and flat – lifeless. She grabbed it into a big pile and shoved it under a bush so she wouldn't have to look at it anymore. She then pulled her bag towards herself and dug through it. She pulled out her sewing scissors, but her pocket mirror was nowhere to be found. She realized she must have left it by the side of her dressing table with her brushes, but she couldn't go back for it now. She put on a hat and stood up. She would fix her hair at the first pond she came across.

She shoved her dress under the blackberry bushes, switched out her cloak for a vest, and pulled on her boots. As she packed up her goods, she realized something else that would need attention – soon.

She had hidden jewels in her pants, but the weight caused the fabric to sag. A lot. She pulled out some twine from the bag and wrapped it around her waist to form a belt.

Satisfied that her bottoms would now stay up, Saphira checked the condition of the rest of her supplies. She had packed light so she could travel faster, but now it seemed pitifully small. It contained food, some more clothes, and a few other essential items. Penelope didn't need much besides grass, and Saphira hoped to be back before winter returned.

With one last glance at her pile's contents, she tied the bag together and took her bundle over to her horse. She tried to distribute the weight evenly on both sides, and after a few minor adjustments, she was ready to set out.

She glanced at the sky. Saphira estimated that the servants were just getting breakfast started. Her absence would soon be noticed. She turned Penelope to face deeper into the forest when she heard a noise. It was low, constant, and rhythmic.

Letting go of Penelope's reigns, she slowly maneuvered herself until she could see what was happening. The wind kept the hair out of her eyes and she could just make out the movement of a search party along the edge of the forest. How did they get here so quickly? Saphira had been counting on at least another hour before they got everyone organized.

Saphira looked at Penelope and was relieved to see her tearing at a patch of grass. Knowing Penelope was quiet when she ate, Saphira shrank against her own bush, preparing to wait them out.

As the men approached, Saphira's legs started to cramp, and her throat itched. She wanted to cough, but fought desperately to suppress it. She focused on breathing in and out through her nose.

How many people did they get? Saphira wondered as the line kept going past her.

It wasn't until everything had been quiet for several minutes that she finally let herself cough. When she was done, she went up to Penelope and patted her on the side. "You did a great job being quiet. We'll find another delicious clump of grass later, but right now I prefer to put as much distance between us and them as I can." Saphira pulled on the bridle, and Penelope reluctantly walked away.

Saphira headed deeper into the forest until she came across another trail. It was small and overgrown, but it was going the direction she wanted to go. Saphira faced

Hallenbreth one last time but couldn't see anything through the thick foliage. That was far enough west for her so she led the horse south.

After several hours of quietly picking her way down the trail, she heard something or *someone* behind her. Her heart raced as she pulled her sword from its scabbard. She ignored the contents of her other bags spilling to the ground and dove into the surrounding bushes. She hoped they would be distracted by the horse and overlook her.

She peeked through the bushes and saw that her pursuer was a single girl. She breathed a sigh of relief. *She must live in the woods*, Saphira thought as she stepped out. Mud was splattered all over her dress, her hair looked like it had been yanked apart by a two year old, and even though she was staring at the horse, her eyes were blank and unfocused. Saphira walked back to her pack and pulled out a loaf of bread. She held it out towards the wild girl but almost dropped it in surprise. "Elena! What happened to you?"

Elena's voice shook as much as her head. "It's gone. It's completely gone."

"What are you talking about?" Saphira demanded as she grabbed Elena's arms.

"Gnomes attacked this morning. Nobody heard them coming. There was no time to respond. I saw them right before they reached my house. They were like a swarm of bees. They were everywhere – filling every street, cutting off every exit." Elena shivered.

"I hid under my bed as soon as I realized they had gotten inside. When they left, I went the opposite direction.

The people I saw..." Elena covered her mouth and closed her eyes as her throat worked to re-swallow what it had spit up. Saphira sat quietly, too desperate to speak, while Elena recovered herself.

"I focused on the trees and ran. It wasn't until I was safely sheltered in their branches that I looked back. They were gathering the survivors in the main square. The gnomes passed torches among themselves and soon every building was on fire."

Saphira turned her head away as she imagined the scene. Her family and friends being tied together, their faces framed with bright orange and yellow licks of flames.

"Who else made it out?" Saphira's voice finally croaked.

Elena shook her head. "No one."

Saphira shook her head and her voice rose with every word. "That's impossible. Someone else *must* have made it. We have to help them." She tried to go around, but Elena grabbed her arm.

"No! It's too dangerous."

Saphira shook off Elena's hands. "I'm going, and you can't stop me." Once free she added, "I have to see it for myself."

Elena bit her lip as she watched Saphira enter the brush. Just before she disappeared, Elena cried out, "Wait for me."

They didn't make it back before night fell. Not willing to risk a fire, they huddled together under Saphira's cloak for warmth. Every sound made Elena jump and sent Saphira grasping for her sword.

When the sun rose the next morning, they were stiff and sore. They spent several minutes packing and reworking the bags so Saphira could easily remove the sword without upsetting the other items on the horse.

All they found on their return was soot and ashes. Except for the occasional black encrusted statue or pillar, everything else had been consumed in the fire. She had never seen flames destroy something so completely.

"What kind of fire did this?" Saphira asked.

Elena shuddered in response. She drew closer to Saphira and stayed there while they searched the rubble. Ash rose with every step they took, and charred sections of wood broke off in their hands when they tried to lift something. It seemed strange to think that these buildings once contained family and friends.

Soon the girls were barely distinguishable from their black and gray surroundings. The occasional charred hand lifted up from the carnage, but it wasn't attached to a survivor. They refused to guess who it might have belonged to.

They can't all be dead. One of these people have to be alive, Saphira told herself. She bit her lip and continued to the next house. Neither she nor Elena spoke as they searched.

It was past noon before Elena declared, "I'm done." She sat down to rest on a pillar that had fallen over. "We've looked everywhere, and haven't found anyone – alive. If they survived, then they aren't here anymore."

"I hate to admit it, but you're right." Saphira joined her.

"Where do you think they took the people they captured?"

Saphira shrugged. "The mines? Where else would they take them?"

"But we're nowhere near the mines. It doesn't make sense."

Saphira gestured around her. "*None* of this makes sense. But it's the only place I know where to look." She resolutely stood up and slapped her pants to get the ash off. "I guess we'll find out for sure when we arrive."

"Where?"

"The mines. If we're at war, then King Cedric won't let his people stay under the gnome's power. He'll find a way to free them if he hasn't already, and we can be there to greet them when they come out."

"But....when did we even start fighting with them?"

"I don't know, but it doesn't matter. We're fighting them now, and we will need to be extra careful until we're back with our own people." Saphira extended a hand and helped Elena stand up. As Elena dusted the ash off her skirt, Saphira added, "Before we leave, there are a few things we need to do first."

Unexpected Answers

Back in the forest, Saphira was waiting for her friend to emerge from some bushes. "How are you doing back there?"

"I don't think I'll be able to do this, Saphira. These clothes are impossible. I feel so… exposed. I don't know how you can stand to wear them — especially breeches! They are so uncomfortable."

"Come out so I can take a look at them. I brought my sewing kit so we can make a few changes to help them fit better."

"Ugh," Elena said as she emerged from the bushes. Saphira burst out laughing. Elena was wearing breeches, a shirt, and a vest like Saphira. Elena had tried to complete the masculine look by twisting her hair up and under a brown hat. Unfortunately, she had nothing to hold it up with so her hair was starting to slide down the sides of her neck. When Elena reached her hand up to fix it as she entered the clearing, she released the remaining tension and the rest of her hair came down in big billowing piles across her shoulders and down her back. But that wasn't what made Saphira laugh so hard.

"Elena, I think I know your problem."

"What?"

Saphira pointed to her waist. "Look at me. Do you see how the buttons are secured in the front?"

Elena looked down and groaned. "I thought they were like Long-Johns."

"No. Go back and put them on correctly. We'll make the rest of the adjustments from there."

After Elena fixed her pants, she was more physically comfortable in her clothes, though not entirely at ease with her new attire. "For the record, I still don't like these. How can men wear these?"

"Don't worry. You'll get used to them in a few hours. They're really much better for traveling."

"Hmm. We'll see about that." As Saphira began putting the extra items back in the bag Elena asked, "How did you end up out here with so many supplies anyway? And what happened to your hair?"

Saphira blushed and handed Elena the scissors, "I'll tell you if you trim it up for me."

Saphira sat down on a large tree trunk. While Elena snipped, Saphira told her about her original plan to rescue Jack.

"What?" Elena stopped snipping. "You were actually hoping to defeat *that*?" Elena pointed towards Hallenbreth, indicating the gnomes.

Saphira shrugged, "Maybe I was being naive, but I had to try. At least it allowed us to start out with some supplies on our journey."

"You're right. It was insane...but it was the perfect thing to do under the circumstance. I should have thought to bring something with me when I ran." She finished the trim and handed the scissors to Saphira.

"I'm just glad you got away," Saphira said as she grabbed the handles. She then stood up and pointed to her vacated seat. "Now it's your turn."

Elena reached back to touch her hair and slowly backed away. "Maybe we should think about this again. I mean, we don't have to be boys. We could be a man traveling with his sister."

Saphira shook her head. "I've thought about it, and it will be safer this way. Besides, I have extra clothes for a boy, but not a girl."

"Then let me try the hat one more time. I'm sure I can get it to work."

Saphira sighed. "We tried that already. It only needs to fail once before we're exposed."

Elena chewed her fingernails as she considered what Saphira had said. "Fine, but at least let me keep some strands."

Saphira agreed and began cutting Elena's hair. When she was done, Elena scooped up some of the longer locks and braided them together to form a ring she placed around her index finger.

"I know I'm being stupid, but I just hate to see it all gone. I feel like I'm giving up on everything that defined being a girl for me: The hair, the dress, the feeling of protection. I guess I just want to keep some reminder of what it was like to be me."

The next morning, the sun shone gently through the trees, and birds chirped merrily. It was peaceful where they lay, and it was hard to imagine that only a few miles away their town lay in ashes.

Saphira pulled out the map and showed Elena where Hallenbreth was. Both the capital and the mines lay to the south. One of the roads leading to the capital followed the edge of the forest for several miles. They would be able to watch it, undetected, as long as they needed to.

Armies and their supply trains would use the roads. If the gnomes had overtaken a town on their route, then they would mark it and move on. Otherwise, they would trade for supplies and information.

Looking at the map, they found a town several miles south that lay close to the road they wanted to follow. Agreeing on that destination as their first stop, Saphira rolled the map back up and put it in her bag.

As she prepared to stand up, she noticed some slender green plants near her hand. She started picking them. "I'll take a couple of these with us. Everything tastes better with fresh onions, don't you agree?"

"Wait, let me smell those," Elena demanded. Saphira handed them over to Elena, confused. Elena sniffed them cautiously before throwing them on the ground.

"What was that for?" Saphira asked as she began to pick them up again.

"Stop! We can't eat those. They are death camas."

"What?" Saphira stared at the stalk in her hand.

"Smell it."

Saphira sniffed one cautiously. "I don't smell anything."

"Neither did I. That's the problem. Onions smell like onions." Elena began to search the ground.

"Aha." Elena pulled up a slender green stalk that looked exactly like the plant Saphira had just picked, except for a small twist at the end.

"Smell this," she said to Saphira, handing it over.

"It smells like onions."

"Exactly."

"But how did you know? I've never heard of death camas before."

Elena rubbed the dirt off her hands before responding. "Do you remember Esau?" she asked.

"He worked in your stables, right?"

Elena nodded. "One day I saw him kissing one of our maids. I could have had him fired, but I said I wouldn't if he taught me how to hunt."

"Why didn't you tell me before?"

"I haven't even told my parents. You know what they would say about a woman hunting, but all I had, *have* are brothers. I wanted to know what all the fuss was about."

"I'm glad you did," Saphira said as she located the real onions and added them to her pack. "Ladylike or not, your knowledge just saved my life."

They travelled back to the southern trail they had met on earlier. It was surprisingly straight and had obviously been built for some purpose, but whoever had made it, stopped using it years ago. Decaying trunks fell across their path and thick shrubs hemmed in their sides. Occasionally, they had to un-strap the horse so they could force her through a particularly narrow channel. Elena was forced to admit that pants weren't all bad.

Along the way, Elena provided fresh rat and squirrel dinners and taught Saphira how to find edible plants. They began to feel more confident in their ability to reach King Cedric, even if they had to hide in the woods the whole time to get there.

"For not having much experience in the woods, you did a good job picking out supplies. I might have changed a few things, but the essentials are here," Elena told Saphira a week into their journey.

Saphira smiled. "You weren't the only one who overheard boys talk about their hunting trips, and Jack was a traveler you know." Saphira's voice lowered. "I miss him so much. I can't believe I actually thought I might be able to help him on my own. Without you, I would have eaten the death camas, and that would have been the end of all my grand schemes.

"You were more prepared for this adventure than I was. If you had chosen the supplies, then we wouldn't need to be so creative with the goods we did bring." Saphira paused and dropped her head. "I was so stupid, and now it's not just Jack's life I'm worried about."

"Stop that!" Elena demanded. "We are surviving. And when the time comes, we can trade some of our smoked foods at a farmhouse for whatever we need."

Saphira lifted her head. "That's right. We can trade, but we have something better to trade with than food."

Elena looked at Saphira confused.

"Money," Saphira said as she ran towards her bag.

Elena watched as Saphira pulled out her sewing scissors and a vest.

"Saphira, you can't turn that vest into money."

"I know, but I did turn money into a vest." Saphira finished picking a small hole in the lining. She slipped in two fingers, pulled out a small bill, and handed it to Elena who looked at it in disbelief.

"What the...? How did you...?"

"I sewed them between the layers," Saphira explained. "I thought it would make it easier to carry and a little warmer at night as well."

"Saphira, you're a genius. I never knew there was anything hidden there. Elena caressed her clothes with more reverence.

"I'm surprised you didn't say anything about the weight. Especially in the pants where I hid some gems. You didn't think they normally slumped like that, did you?"

Elena looked up at Saphira, "After you saw the way I tried to wear them, did you really think I would know how they were supposed to fit?"

Saphira struggled not to laugh. "That's right. I forgot."

Elena quickly changed the subject. "How long before we reach Burkton?"

"Only a few more days, but we'll have to travel east tomorrow if we don't want to miss it."

"I better lead the way, then," Elena said. "Esau taught me some tricks I can use to keep my sense of direction in the forest."

The next morning, they headed towards the road and Burkton. Whatever extra space the trail had provided was gone now. The girls were constantly scratched as they blazed their way through. Some branches had to be yanked off the trees so Penelope could follow them.

They didn't know the forest was about to end until it did. Stepping out into the sun, they gasped and quickly retreated to the shadows. They didn't want to be seen by any patrolling gnomes.

Staying as far in the forest as they could without losing sight of the road, they began to follow it south. When they heard a traveler passing by, they stopped to observe them. Everyone they saw was human and in no hurry. The ones that could be seen spurring their horses on and around the slower caravans weren't dressed for military action.

"I don't know what to make of this," Elena said. "How could the gnomes have gotten to Hallenbreth without causing some sort of reaction in Burkton? Surely they must have heard news of the conflict. Why aren't there more soldiers or guards patrolling the area?"

"The fighting must already be over or at least localized somewhere else. I can't believe our luck. We should still be cautious in case we're wrong, but I'll see if I can get us some more clothes. Traveling, is a lot harder on our clothes than I thought it would be, especially pants."

"While you're doing that, I'll see what they have in the hunting section. If it's not too crowded, then I might be able to negotiate a good price on some new hunting equipment. But I won't care even if it is. I can hardly wait to be in society and surrounded by people again." Elena took a deep breath and then several shorter sniffs. "Although if we can, then we should wash first. We wouldn't want people confusing us with vagrants or...pigs."

Saphira paused and sniffed herself. "Ugh. We do stink. I hope I have enough soap left over to clean more than just our hands and faces before we go in. We will definitely need to pick up some more while we're there."

The next morning, two much cleaner girls tied Penelope to a tree where there was plenty of nearby grass for her to eat before walking into the town. Guards were posted near the gates, but they were relaxed, barely glancing at the people entering the town. The shops were on the street that went right through the middle of town and easy to find. Elena went to the bazaar while Saphira continued on to the enclosed shops. She found the tailor's store and went in.

Inside, a wall lined with bookshelves held bolt after bolt of colorful fabrics. Tables, covered with laces, ribbons, and leathers formed aisles in the middle of the shop. There was even a section of pre-made shirts and pants. Saphira had never seen those before. She excitedly sorted through the pile. If these were the right size, then they would save her a lot of time.

Saphira was holding up some of the sturdier looking pieces against her body when a contemptuous voice asked, "May I help you, sir."

There was something about his tone that she didn't like. She straightened her back and flattened her mouth as she turned her head to look at him. She inched her chin up as she examined the proud man with dark, graying hair. It was smoothed back from his face revealing thin, tight lips. She glanced around the room before replying, "It appears you are the only help in the store today, so I suppose you must." She handed a pile of clothes to the man. "I would like to purchase these items."

As he slowly examined the stack, Saphira's toe tapped impatiently. He divided the clothes into tops and bottoms before saying, "You have an excellent eye. These are some of our finest clothes, but before I wrap them up, may I ask how you are planning on paying for these. I'm afraid that we only accept credit from a few select clients."

The patronizing tone of his voice made Saphira want to punch him, but she needed the clothes. Instead, she swallowed her anger, reached into her pocket and unwrapped a few bills from the pile she had unpicked that morning. Counting the bills, she placed them on the table and said, "This should cover everything."

When the man just stared at the money, she said, "Not interested? Then I guess I will take my money elsewhere.

Good day, sir." She reached for the money, but the man stopped her.

In a much friendlier manner he said, "Wait, no, I think I can give them to you for that price."

Saphira inwardly smiled as she withdrew her hand and his fingers wrapped around the bills.

The tailor put the money in a drawer and came back with some brown paper and twine. He was getting ready to fold the paper over the first shirt when Saphira dumped the rest of the clothes on top. "There's no need to wrap them up separately. Just finish tying them together so I can go."

"Why the rush, young man? Nothing could be that important."

"Yes, it can. I've got to help stop the gnomes. I'm heading south as fast as I can."

"Gnomes?" The tailor looked startled. "What did they do?"

"Destroyed my town."

He shook his head. "I'm afraid one of your friends must be playing a trick on you. I'm sure when you get back home, you'll find your town as safe as ever." He finished tying the string around the four edges of the clothes and secured it with a knot.

"You're wrong. I already went back, and it was gone! It can't have been the only place they attacked. How have you not heard anything?"

The tailor slammed his scissors on the table and said, "What kind of prank are you trying to pull? I promise you I won't fall for it. I have my own friends in the south. They would tell me if the gnomes even tried something like that. They may be low-down, mean creatures, but even you can't make me believe they would go so far as destroy an entire community. We are not at war with them."

Saphira was stunned. "We're not?"

"Not yet we aren't, and we never will be unless people are foolish enough to start believing the lies of troublemakers like you. Now get out of my store."

Saphira grabbed her bundle of clothes as he waved her off. *If we're not at war,* Saphira wondered, *then why did they attack us?*

###

Saphira found Elena purchasing a knife from a stand filled with dozens of other sharp weapons. Some of them had been tied up by their handles to a string that connected the tops of two long poles on the sides of the booth. She didn't like the way the knives swung towards the buyers every time the wind blew so she waited until Elena was walking away from that booth before she joined her.

"Do you like it?" Elena asked, pulling a knife out of its holder. The steel blade was a little longer than her hand and attached to a leather-wrapped handle. "It's the perfect size for most jobs, but he wanted 30 krubes for it! Ridiculous. I finally talked him down to 25 with a whet stone so we can keep it and your sword sharp." She flicked it over in the sun so that its edge caught the light.

"I'm sure that's great, but you will never believe what I just heard." Saphira took a deep breath. "The gnomes are not attacking."

"Then we won!"

Saphira shook her head. "No. It never started."

Elena put the knife back in its holder. "I don't understand. They attacked our town. If we weren't at war before, surely we would have been at war then."

"Not according to the clerk I talked to. He didn't even know about Hallenbreth."

"Then we have to warn them." Elena marched over to an abandoned barrel and stood up. "Good people! Something terrible is happening! You must arm yourselves now, or you will suffer the same fate of Hallenbreth."

People began to gather around Elexa. "What's wrong? What happened."

"It was attacked!" Elena called out and the people gasped.

"Who could have done such a thing?" The crowd murmured among themselves as its size grew.

"Gnomes. They streamed out of the mountain side and attacked when most of our people were still in bed."

"Wait? Isn't Hallenbreth that little tiny town north of here?"

Elena nodded.

"What would gnomes be doing there?"

"Attacking. Killing our people," Elena explained.

Saphira heard the tailor's voice say, "Don't believe them. They are just a pair of warmongers, the two of them.

That boy's companion tried to sell me that same story a few minutes ago."

"It's the truth! I saw them with my own eyes. We have to stop them before they attack again." But the crowd was already dissipating. "Please, you have to believe me. What do you think you are doing? Your town could be next!" But they were already gone.

Elena got down off her podium. "Why didn't they believe me?"

Saphira shook her head. "They didn't want to believe you."

"We have to find a way to make them believe. Maybe if we went back and found proof?"

"That would take too long. We need to go straight to the king."

"And leave these people exposed and vulnerable?" Elexa began to head toward the biggest clustering of people, but Saphira grabbed her arm.

"You already tried; they didn't believe you."

"But the gnomes?"

"Maybe they've already have been caught and punished."

"What if they haven't?"

"That is why we are still going to the king. If he hasn't already learned about our plight and stopped the perpetrators, then we can help him do that. You saw them. You can identify them."

Elena stopped struggling. When she moved again, it was towards the city gates. "Then let's get moving. They will not get away with what they did to Hallenbreth."

Saphira ran to catch up to her.

As they journeyed south, they became better travelers. They could set up and take down their camp sites smoothly and efficiently. They grew comfortable with their disguises, and after a month of losing the occasional knife or meal, they learned how to stop a potential thief from sneaking away with their goods. The caravans they ran into were friendly and more concerned about the threat hostile humans created than gnomes. They told them certain forested areas and towns to avoid and occasionally shared their fire with them for safety against bandits.

As the hills grew taller and steeper, the road swayed away from their bases. The town walls grew thicker, the guards more alert, and the people more wary and purposeful in their travel. As the hills revealed their mountain potential, the trees changed, too. The girls watched with fascination as the broad-limbed, wide-leafed trees from home changed into dark arrowheads covered with sword-like spikes. Eventually, even those proud warriors cowered before the height of the mountains, growing shorter and sparser until only clouds remained to cover the tops.

The mountains were unlike anything they had seen before.

Inspiration

It was getting dark, and they were still half a day's journey from the next town. A group of travelers two miles back had offered to share their fire, but the girls declined. They had run out of cash and needed to pull their gems out of hiding.

After they set up camp, Saphira went to work picking apart a pant seam. Her small needle flashed in the firelight as she carefully spread apart the threads. When she was done, a small collection of jewels cascaded to her feet with soft thuds.

Elena glanced back at Saphira. "I have no idea how you fit all those in one set of pants. I think we can leave the other pair untouched."

"I agree." Saphira nodded as she put her supplies away and began sorting through her gems.

"That one's pretty," Elena said, picking up the diviner. "I don't think I've ever seen a pearl quite like that before."

Saphira looked over at her friend. "It's actually a stone. It represents Langor's diviner. It was the last gift I got from…"

Thinking of her parents brought back the ache she felt for them, and her voice broke. She might never see them again. She wanted to believe they were still alive because she couldn't imagine the alternative. Not when her last note to them had been so callous.

Elena placed the diviner in Saphira's hand and wrapped her fingers around it. "Then I'll do everything in my power to help you keep it." She glanced at the remaining pile. "Do you have any idea how we are going to sell the rest of these?"

Saphira shook her head. She shoved her grief to the side so she could think clearly. "Let's see. We don't have enough gems for a booth, and I know a jeweler would not give us what they're worth..." Her fist tapped against her thigh. "I wish I knew a way to get their full value."

Just as she finished speaking, a spark erupted from the diviner, and Elena gasped. "Did you see that?"

"What?"

"Your stone. It just shot out a beam of light."

Saphira laughed. "Wouldn't that be amazing?" Saphira opened her fist and let the diviner glow with reflected light. She noticed the small pinpricks of extra light that had shone through when she first started her journey and traced them again for comfort. As her fingers moved across its surface, she realized they were making a new pattern tonight. She followed the outline again just to make sure and then laughed.

"What's so funny?" Elena asked.

"I think I just found the answer to our problem."

"What?"

Saphira looked up and asked, "Have you ever heard the story of Drayden and the Pie?"

"No," Elena said, confused.

"One day Drayden needed some money-20 krubes to be exact. He had nothing he could sell except for a pie he had made that morning. He tried to get rid of it all day, but people knew he wasn't a very good cook so they didn't buy it. Refusing to give up, he took the pie back home, put it in a box, and tied it closed with a red ribbon. He then put on an apron and a tall white hat and went to visit the king. He told the king he was a famous chef who had saved his last blueberry pie for the king. If the king wanted it, he could get it for half price, only 20 krubes. The delighted king bought the pie, and Drayden left with his money, grinning from ear to ear."

"Why are you telling me this story?" Elena asked.

"Because that is what we can do. We will pretend to be merchants with only a couple gems left that we want to sell to a few select clients. I remember Jack saying something about how people did that in the South."

Saphira pulled the map out of her bag. Her tongue clicked softly as she skimmed over the notes with her finger. When her finger reached Crishmen, she stopped. "See, look right here. He said they sold goods door-to-door in a town only a few miles south of here. If he can do it there, we can do it here."

Elena eyed the map. "I still have my doubts, but you seem to know more about it than I do. While you try to sell the gems, I'll set some snares and meet you at the town's tavern afterwards."

Saphira went to bed excited about the prospect of trading. After she was asleep, Elena picked through the gems until she found the diviner. She brought it close to the fire's embers. An orange glow lit its surface, but there was nothing...unnatural about the way it reacted to the light. She shrugged her shoulders and returned it to its pile before falling asleep herself.

The next town was more accurately termed a city and had its own permanent outdoor marketplace. The merchants stood behind the booths and called out to passing customers, asking them to examine their seemingly endless variety of goods. Saphira walked along its edges, memorized the name of a busy booth, and then turned towards the larger houses of the rich.

As she moved farther away from the market place, Saphira noticed other traders sending the occasional employee to trade with the home owners and breathed a sigh of relief. So far, so good.

Saphira stopped in front of a large, stone house with arched gateways and landscaping that would require the attention of several gardeners. She took a deep breath before knocking.

The door was opened by a severe looking man in black, fitted clothes. Saphira deepened her voice and said in an accent she had overheard some of the other pages using, "S'cuse me sir, but mig'ten the lord or lady of the 'ouse be interested in buying some jewelry? We 'ave some pieces to sell that we 'ave been keepin for the nicest families." Saphira pulled out a piece of cloth and unrolled it to show him the jewels. They sparkled brilliantly in the sunlight, but the man glanced at them only briefly.

"We don't buy jewels from unsolicited guests, young man."

"But 'ook at the pieces. Your mis'ress 'ould be upset if you passed up such a chance."

"My mistress is not interested in patronizing thieves."

"I ain' no 'ief. I be from Baylor and Sons," she said, using the name of the company she had seen on the way in.

The butler raised his eyebrows. "I didn't realize they now included jewelry among their 'famous smoked goods.'"

Saphira choked as she tried to come up with a response to that, her mouth opening and closing again like a fish. The butler noticed her discomfort and smiled. "You didn't think I'd catch that, did you? I realize the previous butler here might have overlooked such irregularities, but I do not. I'd like to introduce you to one of our under-butlers, Mr. Donnel. Donnel!" A lean, but muscular looking young man opened a door into the hallway. The butler cleared the way to the door and said, "Show our young guest the way to the magistrates' office."

Saphira didn't wait for Mr. Donnel to get anywhere close to her. She closed her fist around the jewels and took off running. She didn't stop until she was safely lost amid the crowd at the marketplace. That had been close. As she tried to calm her breathing, she found the stall that was run by Baylor and Sons and cursed herself for her stupidity. They had sausages, hams, and jerkys, but nothing came close to fine gems or jewelry.

Smarter now, she scanned the bazaar until she found the fine goods. She saw a stall that specialized in high-quality gems and jewels. As she rounded the corner to find its name, she overheard the name of their new apprentice. "That might be useful," she thought to herself as she memorized the information.

Listening to them talk, she realized something else she had done wrong. The owner and his sellers were very careful to enunciate the whole word, like she had been taught in school. Only the farmers, stock boys, and runners, slurred their words like she just had. How could she not have noticed?

Feeling better prepared to impersonate a jeweler, she went back among the houses. Giving the first, disastrous, house a wide berth, she finally stopped in front of a door carved with prancing stags. Taking a deep breath, she knocked hard.

This time she got in.

"It's not often you guys come back here," the mistress said as she looked over the jewels. "This is a better selection than I've seen in a long time." She picked up a sapphire and held it up to the light. "These are lovely and perfect for my new hair pin. I've been trying to match my broach for ages, and now I finally can." The mistress separated the deep-blue gems from Saphira's pile.

"I'll take these. Oh, and this one too," she added as she pulled one last sapphire from the pile.

"You have excellent taste," Saphira said as she wrapped up the rest of her jewels. Settling on a price, Saphira took the money and travelled to the next house. Several hours later, she had sold all but three of the gems she had brought with her.

Elena, meanwhile, had reached the tavern. She met an older woman and her family who had just moved into town. "We cam 'ere because of da gnomes," the woman said. "They're a nasty sort. We used da live in Corbon. Me man and me 'ad our own farm and et was heaven. Den, our son, comes running in from de forest screaming aboud hundreds o' gnomes dressed fir baddle an' marchin' through de forest. We sent a messenger tah da King askin' far protection, an' den we left. We cam 'ere because of de guards. If dey see any of dem, dey shoot 'em.

"Luckily, de gnomes never attacked, bud if dey had, de number of men de king finally sent ta help us would ha' been too few ta do any good. We heard he sent an 'official inquiry' ta de gnomes regarding de matter, and dey said et was a 'scouting trip.' Deh 'regretted' comin' sah near the village an' scaring us, but as for being dressed far baddle, et was nah such thing.

"I dinna believe 'em meself. I believe me kid," the woman inclined her head towards a young man seated beside her, "whos nevah said a lie in his life, over dat Brackster. We ain' nevah goin' back."

"I can't believe the king would have treated your appeal so lightly."

The son shrugged his shoulders and said, "Eh jus' dinna believe us. Bud eveh since dat happened, I've been preparing ta fight. See how strong me arms be naw? I can bea' anyone here in an arm wrestling match."

"Is 'at so," a young farmer asked from the other side of the room. "I'd like ta see ya try and beat me."

Saphira walked into the tavern in time to see a young man stand up angrily from a table and shout at his companion, "Yeh cheated. Eh demand a rematch. Where's de owner? We need ah new table."

"You won' win. But you can try again o'morrow." the farmer seating across from him answered.

"You're on. Yeh won' bead me again."

His muscular opponent laughed at him as he left.

Elena looked over and gestured for Saphira to join her at the table. When she arrived, Elena passed her a cup of mead. "Here, have some. I thought we could splurge a little. How did your trading go?"

"It went well, except I made a horrible mistake at the first house. It's a good thing we aren't staying around much longer. I don't know what I would do if I ran into that butler again." Saphira quickly told Elena what had happened, and then Elena filled her in on what she had learned at the tavern.

"I bet you almost anything that was the group that attacked us," Elena said.

"If it was, then it was a more organized event than we realized. Maybe our town wasn't a random casualty?"

"If that's true, then why did they come? What did they hope to find?"

King Cedric

When they reached the king's city, they still had no answer for why they were attacked, but they knew why the king had not been. The entire city was enclosed behind a gigantic wall. Outside that wall was nothing. No trees, no buildings, not even a stone fence for at least a mile. Nothing could sneak up on this city.

Huge circular towers rose where the corners of the walls met. Between them were several smaller, defensive croppings. There were archers posted atop the walls, and the armored, entrance guards kept a hand on their swords at all times. The city gates were thicker than the girls were tall and reinforced with iron.

"Have you ever seen anything like this?" Saphira whispered to Elena.

"No. It's incredible. Did Jack ever mention the capital?"

"No. I would have remembered if he had said anything about this place. I'll have to ask him what else he neglected to tell me."

As they worked their way into the city, Elena's eyes lingered on the large, windowless buildings marked with signs for grains or weapons. "I wish we had been here when the gnomes attacked. With all these supplies, we could have defended this place for years."

Saphira looked at the buildings Elena pointed out. "At least we'll know our king will be safe if the gnomes declare open war."

They found the castle with ease. It was the largest building inside the walls, and it looked ready to deflect an invading army on its own merits. It had several turrets and long thin windows that let in light and nothing else. Its walls were made from the same stone that was used with the city walls, and the door to the entrance was almost as thick as the walls.

The girls saw the occasional cluster of tradesmen and farmers enter the castle. They joined an old man as he separated himself from the crowd and started towards the castle. "Are you headed inside to see the king?" Elena asked.

"Yes, and do I have a petition for him! Those pesky gnomes have gone too far this time. They constantly steal my cow's milk and hen's eggs, but I would not have come here if they hadn't started taking my onions and turmeric. I need those for my work!"

"Your work?" Saphira asked. "What do you do?"

"I dye clothes, but now I won't be able to make any yellow until next season."

"How do you know it wasn't rabbits?" Elena asked.

"Because of this." He pulled out a purple cloth and waved it at them. "What do you think of that?"

"Umm," Elena said.

He moved the cloth closer to Elena's face and pointed to it. "Tell me you don't see what color this is."

"It's purple," Elena said.

"Purple? Did he just say purple?" The dyer asked Saphira. "This is not just purple. This is *midnight* purple. We can't make this. I can't tell you how many times I have tried, but it never comes out dark enough. Only gnomes can makes this color. This proves they were there."

"Did they take anything else?" Saphira asked.

"Not yet, but I'm going to get the king to stop this nonsense once and for all. I am not some stupid farmer they can take advantage of whenever they want." He put the cloth away. "What's your petition about?"

"They attacked our town," Saphira said, and the man almost choked from joy.

"I knew it! It's not just me. What did they take from you?"

"Everything," Elena said quietly. The man opened his mouth but closed it again when he saw her face.

He turned back towards the castle and was clipped from behind by a plump lady. He stumbled, but the lady didn't look back. He mumbled to himself, "Oh no you don't." He hurried after the passer. He sarcastically said, "Excuse me," as he yanked on her elbow and passed in front of her.

The girls dropped Penelope off at the visitor's stables before going up the broad steps to the castle door. They stepped inside the large hallway and followed the flow of citizens until they formed a line outside a heavily decorated door. The door would open and allow one group in at a time. The girls saw the dyer, still fighting with his nemesis, several groups in front of them.

"So, what did you think of the old man's story?" Saphira asked as they got closer to the door.

"It's really odd. But then I think I've decided that nothing the gnomes have done makes sense. Why attack us? Why take somebody's spices?"

The line moved slowly, and the girls spent their time talking about what King Cedric would do in response to the dyer's request and their own until it was their turn to stand before the king. A guard opened the door and ushered them in. The door shut behind them with a moaning woosh. Armed men completely lined the walls of the room. When Saphira looked back, she saw a guard position himself in front of the door they had entered. The king waited for them at the other end.

They swallowed hard and approached the throne slowly. Now that they were in the same room as the king, they had no idea what to do. Why hadn't they asked somebody what the rules were for making petitions? How should they begin their address? How close should they get? Should they speak first, or let him?

They took their first steps cautiously. Their echoes bounced off the walls and filled the silent room. Every eye but the king's followed their progress. He stared vacantly at the patterned floor in front of him. He had a broad chest and thick arms, but his girth was not imposing. They had expected a warrior whose every move was defined by strength, agility, and action. Instead he slumped against the side of his throne, his head resting on his fingertips. His charisma, if he had any, did not extend past his throne.

Stopping a few feet from the throne, they bowed deeply and King Cedric's eyes focused on them for a brief second before resuming their vacant expression. "Sire," Elena began, "we have come here to warn you of gnomadic aggravations against your fair kingdom." He barely shifted in his seat. "Hallenbreth was attacked without warning. They burned the town and took the survivors."

"Is that so?" the king asked, skeptically. "I haven't received word of any other attacks. What makes Hallenbreth so special?"

"We hoped you might be able to answer that. We only know what they did, not why," Elena said.

The king shifted in his seat.

"If the gnomes took the survivors, then how do you know it was them?"

"Because I escaped. I was at home when they streamed out of the forest and flooded our town. I saw them through my bedroom window, their ears fanned back from their heads as they rushed towards us. Their swords and axes flashed in the morning sun as they smashed doors, crushed windows, and ransacked our homes. I hid until they passed and then ran for safety."

As Elena spoke, Saphira retreated to the same place in her mind she always did when the conversation got too close for comfort. She didn't want to cry in front of the guards. Elena, at least for now, seemed to be in no such danger.

"I passed bodies of family and friends that had tried to stop them. I watched from the woods as the others were gathered like pigs into the town square before the gnomes burned our town down to the ground. The fire was so fast and so fierce, nothing was left standing. I ran into Peter in the woods," Elena cocked her head towards Saphira, "and we came here to warn you."

"Bring me a map!" King Cedric yelled at the guard closest to the door on his left. The guard thumped his fist over his chest before leaving the room.

King Cedric glared at Elena. "You tell your story very well, but we are about to see if there is any truth to your tale."

"You don't believe us?" Elena asked.

"Why should I? Gnomes burn, yes, but not entire towns and not so far away. I know all the border towns, and Hallenbreth is not one of them. You are most likely war mongers hoping to take advantage of the unease people have felt since the last trade went bad."

"How dare you!" Elena clenched her fist, and the guards nearest her took a step closer.

The side door opened, and the guard came back with a map. He handed it to the king who studied it quickly. "Just as I thought," the king smirked. "Hallenbreth is over 600 miles from the nearest gnome border. You lied."

"How can you dismiss our claim so quickly? We warn you that your citizens are in danger, and you aren't even going to send messengers? Go there first, and then accuse us of lying if you can."

"Enough," the king slammed his hand down on the side of his throne. "There is no need to send messengers on a fool's errand."

Cedric flicked his thumb with his teeth, and the girl's arms were suddenly twisted behind their backs. They struggled to get free.

"Take them away where their lies can't upset anyone."

Elena screamed as the guards dragged her from the hall, "What about Corbon? Armed gnomes passed that town. Where were they going?" Elena tried to slam her foot down on the guard's foot without success. As the door shut behind her she yelled, "You have to find out what the gnomes are doing!"

In the hallway, Elena turned her attention to the guards. "Where are you taking us? Don't you *want* to know the truth?"

The guards didn't answer. The girls were led through several hallways and down a flight of stairs before they reached their final destination. The cell door was opened, and the girls were pushed in when they hesitated before the door.

"Not so rough!" Elena demanded, but the guards slammed the door behind them and locked it.

The cell was one of several that lined the wall. It was made mostly of stone, but a small section had been replaced with an iron-bar door that opened into the cell. The far right corner held a small pile of hay and a bucket lay in the corner across from it. Judging from the smell, it was the privy. Saphira toe-inched the bucket as far away as she could.

When the girls sat down on the hay, they heard little squeaks of protest and the scuttling clicks of small creatures moving around to make space for the new occupants.

Elena made a face halfway between crying and smiling, "I'm sorry. I just made matters worse. I hoped to get him to take us seriously, but it didn't work."

"Don't worry. It was the truth. At least we can say that we tried our best."

"But this is not what we hoped for. Instead of trying to rescue our family and friends, we're sitting in a cell, imprisoned by our own king for telling the truth. Who knows how long we'll be here? I would have preferred being in the gnome's dungeon. At least it would make more sense." Elena pulled her knees up and rested her head on them.

"Well, that can still happen," Saphira said. "King Cedric might trade us to the gnomes for other, less 'war mongering' citizens. And if he doesn't, the gnomes could still attack, overtake the castle, and then transfer us to their dungeons."

Elena laughed. "You never give up hope, do you?"

"Of course not."

The girls sat in the dungeon so long the days began to merge together. They tried to track the time, but they couldn't even be sure they got fed three times a day. The swill they were given came up almost as often as it stayed down, and they had to huddle together on the hay to stay warm.

They wondered how much longer they would be there and what was happening in the main part of the castle. Had the king sent a messenger to their town? What had they seen? Were there any other gnome attacks?

They tried to ask the guards, but they never spoke. Their faces were impassive and gave nothing away as to what might be happening outside. They had almost given up hope of an answer when a guard passing them their food whispered quickly, "I believe you."

Escape

"What?" Saphira asked.

"Shh." The guard looked around before leaning closer to the bars. "The gnomes. I believe you. I was there when you presented your petition to the king. He never sent messengers, but I did. You seemed so certain. I wanted to find out for myself. Their reports backed up what you said."

"Thanks. I would say I'm glad, but I still wish it was just a horrible nightmare," Elena said. "What will the king do now?"

The guard grimaced. "Nothing. I tried to tell him, but he won't listen. I know better than to press the issue. He does not want to admit that relations with the gnomes might be deteriorating. He hates the thought of war. As long as the gnomes give him an excuse, he does nothing."

"So what happens now?"

"I get you out of here. You told the truth, you should not be in this pit." He spat the last word out.

"But how?" Elena asked as she walked to the bars. "You said the king won't listen to you."

"With these." The guard held up some keys, and Saphira joined them. As he unlocked the door, he cautioned them, "We need to hurry. Our absence will soon be noticed."

"Our? You're coming with us?" Elena asked as she stepped into the hallway.

"I have to. You'd never make it out of here if you tried to use the doors. I can show you a back way out."

"The king will know you helped us."

"Possibly, but I'm not going to change my mind now. Here, put these on. I stole them from the guard house, and you will need these to move around the castle undetected." He handed them two helmets and cloaks that went to their feet.

"Why are you doing this?" Saphira asked.

"Because it's my duty. You performed yours, and now it's my turn." He helped them get their helmets strapped on correctly and paused while he was working on Elena's.

"You're not very old are you?" he said.

"I'm old enough," Elena said, jutting out her chin.

"You wouldn't think it to look at you, or hear you."

"Are you done criticizing? I'd really like to leave before somebody sees us." Elena angled her head towards the exit.

The guard nodded. "Yes, of course. Follow me. Stay close behind, like you're flanking me, and don't say a word to anyone." He led them down the hallway and up a flight of stairs until they were back in the main part of the castle. From there, he took them along several smaller hallways until they stood in front of a plain, unmarked door. He opened it and ushered them inside. It was a small study with a long narrow window against the wall. The thin light shone over a highly polished wooden desk and chair set that had a quill and piece of paper laid out on it. Across from the desk stood an empty fireplace.

The girls were surprised to see him cross over to the fireplace and get down on his hands and knees in front of the hearth.

"What are you doing?" Elena hissed.

"Shh," he said, pointing his finger back to the door. He then turned his attention back to the hearth and wiped off the bottom left corners of the foundation stones. One of the stones' corners was smoother than the others. He reached under its base, and the stone lifted up into his hands. Underneath it was a narrow tunnel leading down.

He motioned for the girls to come over, and he helped them into the tunnel. Elena went first and Saphira followed. As her hands touched the cold, chalky walls, she shuddered. This was ten times worse that the dungeon had been. The guard urged her forward, and she cautiously stepped into the darkness. The silence was broken by the scrapping of the stone closing shut, sealing them into this pit. She began to scream, but the guard's hand quickly covered her mouth.

"Do you want to get us all caught? Keep your mouth shut and go forward."

Saphira struggled to follow his advice. He was with them, and he wouldn't have trapped himself in a pit to die. But it was hard to believe that this tunnel was ever going to end.

They travelled as fast as they could in the darkness, and were eventually rewarded as the tunnel began to lighten.

"I can see the exit," Elena whispered.

The guard urged them forward, and the path widened as it got lighter. When they were almost at the exit, the guard moved forward to take the lead. They walked forward into a chasm that still shielded them from immediate view. After a quick peek over the top, the guard came back down.

"We're good to go. Follow me and move as quickly as you can."

The guard climbed his way to the top, and the girls scrambled after him. He then ran towards a small clump of bushes in front of him and the girls followed. He continued on, crouching through the thigh-high bushes until he reached a clearing framed by a small semi-circle of dirt colored rocks. The guard finally took off his helmet, and settled against the back of a rock. Sandy blond hair framed a broad face.

"We can rest here for now," the guard said.

The girls nodded and found their own seats.

"How did you know about the tunnel?" Elena asked.

The guard shrugged. "I grew up here. I had heard there were secret passages hidden throughout the castle, and I was determined to find them all. That room used to be where they would send me when I had gone too far - until I discovered its secret. It drove them crazy trying to figure out how I had escaped. I came here until I was ready to go back. That reminds me..." The guard leaned over and pulled up a smaller looking rock. He then used it to dig into the earth below it until he unearthed a small box. He opened it to reveal a blanket, some crackers, a canteen, and a few other essential camping supplies. He handed the food and water to Elena.

"The food might be stale, but it's safe to eat. We can refill the canteen when we get to the river."

"How far away is that?" Elena asked, biting into a cracker.

"Not far. We should reach there by tonight. From there we can follow it to a friend's house. He'll keep you safe until we determine our next move."

"We already know our next move," Saphira said, taking the food from Elena. "We're going to the mines."

The guard's head snapped in Saphira's direction. "No. It's too dangerous." He turned back to Elena, "You can't seriously be thinking about going there on your own. You'll never make it. If I had known you wanted to spend your days in a prison cell, then I would have left you where you were."

Elena looked at him straight in the eye. "We have to try. It's our family down there. If the king won't do anything, then we must. We're not as helpless as we look. We made it all the way down here just fine."

"In human territory. This would not be the same. You would need more people to have any chance of success. Listen, I can help you. I have contacts with people who might be willing to fight. If you tell them your story..."

Elena shook her head. "You were the only guard we got to acknowledge us. When they find out the king refused to do anything, they'll reach the same conclusion he did."

Now it was the guard's turn to shake his head. "Not all of them. Believe me, they were listening when you spoke. They couldn't talk to you, but they've talked about it with the other guards. You had more supporters than you realized; they were just too scared to do anything about it."

"If they were too scared to act then, why would they act now? Especially against the king." Saphira's shoulders slumped. "We came to the king to warn him, but he is right. We have no proof except our word. If the evidence was as undeniable as we thought, then he would have acted. Maybe if we can free at least one of our townspeople…."

The guard slung his fist down. "There isn't time. The gnomes are getting ready for something. They won't be at peace with us for much longer. We should start mobilizing an army now."

Elena raised her hand. "No. If the gnomes were actively on the move, then we would have to do whatever we could to stop them, but they are not. It is the king's job to wage war. My father taught me that unity is the key to strength. Without the king's support, we will be divided before we even begin. That won't help."

"But if he doesn't come around before they attack, then that would put us at a great disadvantage. *Some* force, even if it *is* divided would be better than nothing." He said, failing to even glance at Saphira during his last speech.

"Then you would have to be on defensive, familiar ground," Elena spat back, eyes narrowed at the guard. "For your best chance to defeat them, they would have to come to you. But while you're waiting, our friends and family are suffering. If we succeed, then you'll get the evidence you need. If we fail," Elena choked, and continued in a quieter voice, "If we fail, at least we wouldn't be a large enough group to frighten the gnomes into launching a full-scale counterstrike. Hopefully, you'll get the evidence you need before that happens."

Saphira put her hand on Elena's shoulder. "And don't worry about us. Even in the mines, at least we'd be with our loved ones again." Both girls' eyes filled with tears, as Elena nodded solemnly.

The guard shook his head slowly. "I still think you're making a huge mistake, but I can't let you go in there completely unprepared. I'll teach you everything I know about gnomes and their mines. If you manage to make it out of there, then find me in Devis."

"You're going to help us?" Elena asked, surprised.

"I have to. You were right about the need for unity, and the more information we have, the better. I just wish I could think of a better way to get the evidence I need to prove they are preparing for war."

"We can't thank you enough for your help," Saphira said. "But we've never been formally introduced. I am Peter, and this," she said, pointing to Elena, "is my friend Stephen."

The guard nodded to each of them before pointing to himself. "I'm Jillian."

"Were you named after the prince?" Elena asked.

Jillian shook his head. "No, after the Jigglin' Lamb."

Elena laughed. "Are you serious?"

Jillian shrugged his shoulders. "It was my mother's favorite dish."

Saphira joined in the laughter then, and it was several moments before the girls calmed themselves again.

"If you two are done, then let's get going. I've think we've rested enough for now."

The girls nodded and Jillian quickly reburied the box with the blanket inside. They had already finished the crackers, and Saphira held the almost-empty canteen. Jillian led them through the brush, and they reached the drying river bed as twilight descended.

"We'll stay here for tonight," Jillian said, looking around. There wasn't enough room for them all to be together, so they each found their own hiding space by the bank and promptly fell asleep.

By the time Saphira woke up, Jillian had a small, smoke-less fire going, and Elena was placing some frogs over a spit to cook.

Saphira walked over groggily. "Where do we go now?" she asked as she sat down.

Jillian pointed west. "We'll follow this river downstream for the next several days. It won't take you straight to the mines, but at least we won't need to worry about getting lost or running out of water."

Saphira looked at the rivulet of water next to her and said, "Are you sure about that? I feel like we could lose this water any second."

"Don't worry. Even in this dry season, the water never completely goes away."

Saphira took his word for it, and soon they were eating a hearty breakfast. Before they left, Jillian quickly made Elena and him a bow and some arrows. They scouted ahead, looking for game to catch along the way while Saphira followed, gathering dry kindling and refilling the canteen after each water break.

That night they stopped early enough to make a decent camp. While their dinner of squirrel meat and rabbit was cooking, Jillian told them about the gnomes. He told them the types of areas they liked to ambush people at and all the known routes to their kingdom in the dirt for them. He even taught them how to say "Hello," "Goodbye," and "Attack" in Gnome.

"I *suppose* those are good words to know," Elena commented. "At least we'll know when to run."

Jillian laughed. "I wish I knew more, but they don't speak it much around outsiders. I know they can be extremely quiet when they want to be and those that escaped their attacks usually saw them before they heard them. They are very quick, and their intelligence should not be underestimated."

The girls fell asleep to that sober thought.

The next night Jillian and Elena were laying snares for the next day. Jillian was holding up a rock while Elena baited the trap. As he looked down at her hand he said, "That's an interesting ring you wear on your finger. I've never seen anything quite like it."

"This?" Elena looked down at her finger. "Let's just say it reminds me of a girl I used to know."

"You must have been close."

Elena smiled. "The closest." She finished smearing the trigger and stood up.

Jillian released the rock and the trap held. Nodding in satisfaction they moved further away from camp. Jillian asked. "What happened to her?"

Elena bent down and examined a small opening under a bush that might be part of a rabbit path as she said, "I haven't seen her since the gnomes attacked our town."

"Is that why you are so determined to go? Are you hoping to find this girl again?"

"That's part of the reason." She held up her hand, and Jillian passed her a small, knotted cord.

"She must have been pretty special," he said.

Elena looked up at Jillian. "I thought she was," she said, and then she turned back to finish her work.

"Do you think you'll marry her?"

"What?" Elena accidentally set the snare off. "Curses," she said as she bent down to set the trap again. "Sorry, but no. It wasn't that kind of love. I just worry about her, about all my family. Who knows what will be left of them when this is all over?"

"Don't worry, you will be reunited soon. Although, hopefully it will be out, instead of inside, the tunnels."

"That's the plan." Elena stood up and dusted her pants. "Maybe I'll introduce you to her when this is all over."

"I would like that."

Elena paused. "Me, too."

Saphira then called them back to eat.

After Jillian was satisfied that they knew everything he knew about the gnomes, the topics began to wander at the evening fire.

"Stephen used to host the best parties," Saphira declared one night. "Everyone would talk about them for days."

"Really? This is something you're proud of?" Jillian took a bite of squirrel before facing Elena. "I thought party planning was more of a girl's specialty."

Saphira almost choked on her water, but Elena replied easily. "That's what you say until you go to a party where no thought was spent on entertainment. A few hours of being bored crazy quickly teaches you how essential that skill is for anybody to learn."

"You might have a point there." Jillian shuddered. "I'm starting to have flashbacks of our state functions. I just thought it was the company that made them so dull. I never realized there was a science to it. You will have to teach me some of your secrets to success."

"I will," Elena agreed, "but only if you teach me about those rocks I saw you start the fire with tonight. I've never seen it done that way before."

"What? You don't know how to start a rock fire? It's an essential skill that everybody should know," Jillian said in mock horror.

Elena put her plate down and licked the last bit of food from her fingers. "Then our trade will be even – one essential skill for another."

Jillian laughed. "You have a deal." He put his own plate down and shook her hand.

Their last night before they had to separate Jillian told them more about their king. "He's a good man at heart, but he is not a soldier and thinks he can avoid fights through intimidation. That's why he has so many buildings set aside for weapons and 'siege' foods. Most of them are empty, but only a few people know that.

"It's also why he has so many guards with him in the petition room. He wants to stop assassination attempts before they start. That technique also keeps most people from even complaining." He glanced at Elena. "You have to be very brave to confront the king in that room."

"Why is he so scared?" Saphira asked. "Has anyone actually ever tried to kill him?"

Jillian nodded. "Unfortunately, yes. And when they're willing to sacrifice their own lives, it makes them incredibly hard to stop."

"And you're worried that the gnomes are going to start their own attempts to kill us?" Elena asked, and he nodded his head again.

The next morning, the girls were genuinely sad to see him divide up their last few items. He was fun, open, generous, and more concerned about the kingdom's welfare than his own.

"It's not too late to change your mind and come with me," Jillian reminded them. "Your fervor especially, Stephen, would go on a long way towards helping convince people of the danger they face."

Elena looked torn, but Saphira shook her finger. "Don't tempt us. We really wish we could take you up on your offer, but we can't abandon our town." Elena nodded her head in agreement.

"I know, but I had to try one more time." Jillian continued to look at her, and Elena finally transferred her gaze to her feet. Jillian continued, "Whatever happens, I'm glad you forced me to realize the danger gnomes pose. I wish you two the best of luck. Your devotion and bravery are commendable." Jillian thumped his chest and bowed his head towards them. "I hope I can find other people with your determination to do whatever it takes to protect others from injustice."

"I'm sure you will," Elena said as the girls returned his salute. He left, and the girls turned to face the mountains alone.

Dragons

The day after Jillian left was a long, lonely one for the girls. After he left, Elena had a hard time focusing and was easily distracted. Every time there was a crash behind them, Elena would spin around with a smile, only to let it fade when there was nothing there. Even Saphira was disappointed that Jillian hadn't changed his mind and decided to go with them. As night settled, Saphira became determined not to let herself or Elena think about Jillian. Holding up a small topaz jewel, she said, "Elena, there is still a village between us and the gnomes, do you want to go on one last trading trip before we cross over?"

Elena gasped. "I forgot all about those."

Saphira smiled at how well her plan was working. "So did I, until this one fell out while I was stacking the wood for the fire."

"Did any more jewels fall out?"

Saphira began tearing at the hidden seams. "I don't think so. I hope not." When the last gem clinked on top of the pile Saphira heaved a sigh of relief. She picked it up and held it to her chest.

Elena looked up from her tinder box and said, "Is that your diviner?"

Saphira nodded and smiled at her rock. "I was beginning to get worried. I know it's not the real thing, but I feel like it helps me sort things out, and there are so many things I don't know the answer to. How do we get in? How will we get out? How will we find Jack and the others?...It's almost like having my parents around again."

Elena gestured to the guide, and Saphira held it out again. "How can we succeed?" she whispered.

The light from the fire began to illuminate it, and the deep pinpricks she had begun to expect when she asked it a question emerged. Saphira traced the dots. Frowning, she traced them again. She turned the guide around and traced the points another way. It wasn't working. Before, the sparkles reminded her of a constellation whose connected stories gave her the answers she sought, but this time, it was just dots. If it was a constellation, it wasn't one she was familiar with.

She was trying one last combination when a raspy voice whispered, "I would put that away if I were you." She almost dropped the diviner in surprise. "Elena!"

But when she looked over, she realized it wasn't her. Elena's knuckles were white where they grabbed a knife that wasn't in her hand a few seconds ago. Her body lay in a low crouch, and she stared at the surrounding void intensely.

"Show yourself," Elena demanded.

"Do you really think you can order me?" the voice responded, laughing slightly. "Meet me at the Northern Cave but don't touch the shakra again until you arrive. I won't be able to protect you if it becomes known what you carry."

"How can we trust you?" Elena asked, still looking for the source of the sound.

This seemed to amuse the voice immensely. "You can't, but I am not the most dangerous thing in these mountains. I, at the most, would only kill you."

"Oh, good," Elena muttered.

"You have one week. Head south. When you see it, you will know."

"But how?" Saphira waited before asking, "How will we know?" She waited a few minutes before she shouted one last time, "Are you there?" But nothing answered her cries.

Elena lowered her knife. "What do you make of that?" she asked Saphira.

"I don't know? But if there's a fate worse than death, then I don't want to experience it." Saphira put the diviner away.

"I wish we did have a shakra. I wonder what he was talking about?"

"Maybe he thought it was my diviner, but I don't see how he could make that mistake. My diviner is no more deadly than a rock."

"What should we do now?"

"I don't think we really have a choice. It sounds like we're going to the Northern Cave. Maybe we can trade the 'shakra' for help rescuing our friends. At least it's the direction we were going anyway," Saphira said.

"But how will we even find *his* cave? There must be dozens if not hundreds in these mountains."

Saphira shrugged. "If he really wants us to get there, then he'll arrange a way for us to find it."

Two days later Saphira and Elena walked into a small village. It was just a few houses clustered together. The houses had well-kept wooden roofs and their stone walls had fresh grout even though the stones themselves had rounded with age. Elena pointed to the smokeless chimneys and quiet barns. Elena gingerly pushed a door open and peeked inside. "It's empty."

"That's odd. Where is everybody? You don't think the gnomes got them, do you?"

Elena pointed to the one house that wasn't quiet. "Let's go find out."

They walked quietly to its borders, careful to stay in the shadows as much as they could. They saw a plump older lady walk out of the barn just as they arrived. She carried a bucket filled with fresh cream in her hands and started walking back to the house. Elena shifted positions, and the woman stopped. She turned around and said, "Good gracious children, what are you doing there? Why you're skinnier than chickens in a drought." She set her bucket down and grabbed their arms.

"You come inside right now, and eat something." She led them to the kitchen before going back for her bucket.

For several seconds the girls just sat there and breathed. The room was heaven for the nose. Everything smelled delicious. Whiffs of fresh baked bread mingled with assorted spices and herbs. But the best odor emanated from the pot over a small fire against the far wall.

Saphira's stomach growled ferociously in response. The woman returned just in time to hear. She laughed as she set her burden against the wall. "Don't worry, I heard you." She shooed them towards the table and went to get them some food. She returned with a bowl of stew and a fresh roll for each girl. "There, now eat. There's no need to be polite."

"Thank you," the girls managed to say before they filled their mouths with the warm food. It tasted as good as it smelled. "Mmm. This is so good," Elena said in near ecstasy. She finished her meal much faster than was polite, but the old woman just smiled when she saw it was gone and refilled it for her. "Would you like some more as well?" she asked Saphira.

"Yes, please."

The woman grabbed her bowl and gave her another helping as large as the first one. "It's a good thing I made extra. I'd almost forgotten how much young men can consume. So tell me what are you doing out here? We don't get many visitors anymore."

"We're hunting. My friend and I were following a promising deer trail. It got away, but we came across your village on our way back to camp. It would have been a beauty.

Its hoof prints were bigger than my hand." Saphira held her palm up.

"I'm sorry about my stomach's bad manners earlier," Saphira continued. "It had just been awhile since I had smelled anything so good. Neither my friend nor I cook anything so delicious."

"Well, it's not to be expected. You don't spend your whole day in the kitchen, do you?"

"No, especially not lately."

"Well, that's the difference. I have had a lot more practice than you have. Would you want any more? I had two boys of my own. They've long since gone off on their own, but I remember that they were always hungry, especially after a long hard day in the fields or after hunting." The old lady smiled fondly at the memory. "But here I am drifting off to the past that's of no interest to anyone here but myself."

"How long have you lived here?" Saphira asked.

"Longer than I care to admit. I was born and raised in that farm over there, got married and moved to this house, and I have been here ever since. The ground is fertile and the views are amazing."

"If you don't mind us asking, then where's everybody else?"

The woman sighed. "They got scared. It's too close to the gnomes, and the mountains can be a bit oppressive for some." The woman looked down at the empty bowls. "Would you like some more?" she asked. The girls shook their heads.

Their host continued to talk as she took their dishes away. "My parents used to try to scare me away from those hills by telling me scary stories about flesh-eating dragons and immortal gnomes who want nothing better than to snack on the bones of children who stray too far into the mountains. However, we were able to maintain a good sized village here until just recently."

"What happened?" Elena asked as the woman put the dishes in a sink.

The woman looked out the window above the sink and sighed. "A yellow fog drifted down from the mountains."

Saphira looked at Elena. A *yellow* fog?

"We have seen some strange things in our days, but that scared most people right silly. I tried to tell them it was just smoke, but they wouldn't listen. They said it smelled of death. They were certain it was poisonous and would kill us all. People who had never believed any of the local legends suddenly took them very seriously. They left with their families as soon as they could." She shook her head at the memory.

"Why didn't you leave?" Saphira asked.

She turned back to them and smiled. "These mountains are my home. I know by heart every section of these woods. If any creatures did come down off the mountains looking for me, then I could give them a few surprises they weren't expecting."

"Dragons? Immortal gnomes? Do you really believe such things exist?" Elena asked.

"I think there's rumor enough to support both those ideas. We know gnomes live a lot longer than us. Who knows how much longer? They certainly might seem immortal in our eyes. As for dragons…I don't think that idea is so impossible.

"There are strange things that happen around our village, and they have nothing to do with gnomes. Birds never fly above the trees here, and no big-game hunting expedition that goes west of our borders has ever been successful. All the tracks disappear, and an oppressive silence descends around you, like someone is watching you.

"Local legend blames it on dragons. They have their own place in the stars called the dragon's plane. Most constellations are marked by stars, but ours is marked by the lack of stars. It looks like a long black trench has been dug out of the sky. We claim it's where the dragons go to feed."

As the old lady spoke, Saphira remembered what her guide had shown her. She had struggled to place it before, but now she knew exactly what it was. It was the dragon's plane. She leaned in closer.

Elena's eyes darted towards Saphira. Her voice trembled as she asked, "Do you think there really are such things as dragons?"

The old woman joined them at the table. "I do. My neighbors used to laugh at me, but there are so many stories of them, they have to be based on something. Dragons possessed incredible powers. We only know a small number of things that they could do. To imagine that we, who have no powers, could outlast a race that had so much magic is crazy.

"My friends and I liked to pretend that we had one living in the Northern Cave, and that's why the gnomes didn't bother our particular town. Gnomes are even more scared of dragons than we are. And for good reason, if the stories are true."

Elena glanced sideways at Saphira who remained focused on the speaker.

"The cave is too small to house an actual dragon, of course, but those who are brave enough to visit its edge say it doesn't feel right. They say hatred oozes around its edges like the stench of rotten eggs, and its mouth is darker than the blackest night, stopping even the sun's rays from penetrating inside. No one has actually been brave enough to go inside."

"Where is it?" Saphira asked.

"Just beyond the lake. It lies straight up the mountains from here." The woman pointed out the window. "We would swim there during the summer."

"Weren't you scared the dragon might eat you? I don't know much, but I thought they were meat-eaters. What would stop them from snacking on one of you?" Elena asked.

"I don't think anything could, but they never ate humans. I'm sure you've heard the tales of them capturing princesses and carrying them back to their lair, but they are always alive when the prince finally got around to rescuing them. If they were for food, then why target royalty anyway? It would be much easier to pick off a peasant working in the fields or some lone traveler.

"I believe they are like crows, attracted to things that are bright and colorful. It's why they targeted princesses in their rich attire and why they let the knights in their shiny armor get as close as they did.

"Some believe that was the dragons' only, or at least it was their biggest, weakness. However, since princesses walk around freely, I believe the surviving dragons must have found a way to control those urges."

"This is so interesting. How do you know so much?" Saphira asked.

"Let's just say I was fascinated as a youth. I could never hear enough about dragons. Whenever someone new would pass through town, I would always ask them if they had anything they could add to my knowledge. Sometimes I would get lucky, and the stranger would have lots of stories to tell. They almost always lived by the mountains themselves, where tales about dragons are more common."

"You remind me of someone I knew," Saphira told her. "He loved hearing about the local legends and heroes. I wish we had some dragon tales of our own to share with you, but we don't know any."

"Oh, don't worry about that. I've got too many already."

The girls got up from the table. "Thank you so much for your hospitality and the wonderful meal. We haven't enjoyed ourselves so much in a long time. Would you accept something in repayment?" Elena took out a bright green emerald from their store of jewels and held it out to her. The woman's eyes flashed yellow, and her fingers jumped out to grab it, but she controlled herself before the girls noticed. She laughed and waved the gem aside.

"Posh. Don't insult me. It was a pleasure."

"Then would you accept it as payment for some more of your food?" Saphira asked. "Your stories were so interesting we almost forgot our original reason for coming here."

"Of course I will, and I'll even throw in a few extra fish hooks for you in case you visit our lake. But you don't need to worry about paying me for them, I'm just glad for the extra company. I miss the other villagers who used to live here." She bustled out of the room and returned a few minutes later with a big bag that she proceeded to fill with several loaves. She then handed the bag over to the girls. "Everything is inside. I hope you two have a safe journey and find another big buck to rival the one you lost."

"Thank you, but you are much too generous. We couldn't possibly take all this."

"Nonsense. I have a tendency to cook too much, and I know you two will enjoy it much more than the rats."

"Thanks again," the girls said as they stood up to leave. Once they were back outside, Elena looked at the mountains and the woods again. "Are you sure you want to do this? I'm beginning to have second thoughts. It's one thing to take on gnomes, but dragons? We know so little about them."

"So you think it might have been a dragon, too?"

"I don't know what else it could be. It would certainly explain a few things, but I'd rather not be eaten by anything if I could help it." Elena shivered.

"The lady didn't seem to think that we would be in any real danger of that."

"Yes, but maybe he was just smart enough not to eat the locals. No one would know, or care, if we went missing. If he's been in hiding for the last hundred plus years, then who knows what he has been living on? We might look really tasty to him."

"Yes, but thanks to that woman's generosity, we have bread and some jewels left. If he tries to eat us, then we can offer him something else instead."

"If he's that hungry, then I don't think he could be distracted by a few shiny jewels or slices of bread."

"Then we could always suggest some yummy gnomes." Saphira smiled at her friend.

"Unless he reached out to us, because he *had* been eating gnomes and finally got sick of them. We would be a soft, delicious meal that practically walked into his mouth." Elena slowed her steps down.

"We're not so soft anymore." Saphira grabbed Elena's arm and kept walking. "I don't know why you are so worried. One dragon can't be worse than a legion of gnomes, and you were ready to face them."

"Yes, but I didn't think they'd eat me. That is not how I pictured myself dying."

"If he tries to eat you, then you can say, 'I told you so,' but I don't think he will. I actually feel more confident about this decision since hearing about the dragon's plane."

"That makes you *more* comfortable?" Elena gasped.

Saphira nodded her head. "Yes, because I recognized the section of the sky she was talking about. When I was looking into the diviner the night we heard the voice, I thought I saw that void reflected in the globe. I couldn't name it before, but that must have been it. I think it's a sign that we should go there. And if he is a dragon, then he would be very powerful, and we could get a lot farther with his magic and knowledge than we could alone."

"Fine, we'll go, but if he starts to look hungry, then he gets to eat you first."

A Second Encounter

The ground was rising quickly before them. As they climbed, Saphira realized that they had done it. They had made it all the way to the mountain, and soon they would have an ally to help rescue Jack and the others. What would their reunion be like? She would give a surprised gasp and there would be lots of tears and fierce hugs with her parents, if they were still alive, but what about Jack?

As Saphira passed under a particularly thick section of branches, she pretended its dim light was the result of flickering torches planted in crevices along the rock walls. She moved silently, careful not to let her sword click against its hard edges. There in the distance lay the cells.

She snuck over to where they held Jack. The keys rattled slightly, but it wasn't until the door rasped open on its hinges that he looked up. He rubbed his eyes and stared at her in disbelief, "Saphira? How did you get here?" He wanted to hold her hand, smell her hair, and touch her face to reassure himself that she was real, but she urged him on. "Come quickly, we have to go." He followed like a man in a daze until they both reached safety and collapsed into each other's arms.

But then Saphira remembered her short hair and masculine clothes. He might not recognize her. "Who are you?" Jack whispered as she opened his cell. "Saphira," she answered, urging him out. He followed, disbelieving, until they were outside, and he saw her in the sun for the first time. "What happened? You used to be so pretty, and now…"

"It will grow back," she reassured him, but he shook his head. "I'm sorry. We will always be friends, but I can never think of you the same way again. Whenever I think of you, I will see you as a boy."

"Please, I love you. You can't let it end like this. Not after all I've gone through."

Jack shook his head. It was too late.

Too late to even make it out of the mines safely. She and Jack were headed to freedom when a gnome surprised them. They separated, each one taking a different tunnel. Lost in the twisted honeycomb mines, Saphira used her nose, turning wherever she sensed the lightest, freshest air. She started moving too fast and tripped over a rock. It caused other rocks to come lose, giving away her position. One of them sliced into her hand as her exhausted body struggled to get back on her feet.

"Ouch," Saphira cried out as the pain became real and not just imagined.

She tried to step back from the fantasy she had created but couldn't. It took on a life of its own. She was panting heavily, her lungs ached, and she was aware of an overriding fear that cried, "It's not safe. I have to get out of here."

Bursting into the open sun, she was temporarily blinded, but continued to press away from the cave. She didn't have much time. The others would follow soon. She stumbled through the scratching branches, constantly moving north, until she reached another cave. There were claw marks along its sides that vibrated with an intensity she had never experienced before. The edges of the cave flowed in and out as a tide of power washed over them.

She had arrived at the Northern Cave. She had made it...she hoped.

Glancing over her right shoulder, she didn't see any enemies, but she did catch a glimpse of a lake behind her. She turned back to the cave, but the details began to blur and fade behind the real landscape. Saphira looked around and blinked her eyes several times. She wasn't sure how long the experience had lasted, but Elena was no longer anywhere in sight. "Elena! Where are you?"

"I'm here," Elena's voice drifted back.

Saphira sighed in relief. She hadn't fallen too far behind. She moved towards Elena's voice. "Do you see the lake anywhere?"

"Not yet, but we've got to be close. It can't be that far from the village if the woman used to swim there. If I climb one of these trees, then I might be able to see it."

Saphira heard leaves shake as Elena climbed up a tree. After a few minutes, Elena called down, "I see it. It's straight ahead of us." Saphira reached the tree as Elena jumped the last few feet to the ground. A few minutes later they arrived at the water's edge.

The lake sparkled in the sun like a giant sapphire. Saphira scanned the mountain for the cave from her vision while Elena dropped her bag and reached for the water. The cool liquid covered her hand and spilled down her throat when she lifted it. Saphira joined her, and more body parts joined the hands until they were completely submerged, laughing and splashing each other. They let the refreshing, clean water work its way through their hair and under their clothes to get their backs and shoulders.

"This feels so good. I haven't felt this clean since....I don't know when," Saphira said.

"And our clothes are getting cleaned at the same time. Double glory."

After swimming for a few more minutes they got out and found a sunny spot to lie down while the sun dried their clothes.

"This is wonderful." Elena sighed contentedly. "I can see why the old lady loved to come here. I wish we had a lake like this at home. I don't know how it stays so clear."

"It's just one of the mysteries of the mountains," Saphira replied.

Elena flipped onto her back. "I wish we could stay here forever, but we'll have to head to the cave eventually. Do you see it anywhere?"

"It's west of here, about two miles away."

Elena looked over where the cave should have been and shielded her eyes. "I don't see it anywhere. You have great eyesight."

Saphira shook her head. "It's not that. I can't see it either from this angle."

"Then how do you know it's there?"

Saphira began plucking the grass by her head. "This is going to sound weird, but as we were walking here, I thought about what it would be like to actually be inside the caves. Suddenly, the image took on a completely different tone, or feel. I was no longer in control. I was led out of gnome's shafts and taken to the Northern Cave. It is small with long thin marks along its edge, but there is something not quite right about its entrance. I can't explain it, but there is some magic at work there."

Elena rolled onto her side to face Saphira. "Has anything like that happened to you before?"

Saphira shook her head and turned towards Elena. "I wonder if it is somehow related to the dragon? Maybe that's why he was so confident we'd be able to find it."

"Either way, I'm glad you had to deal with it and not me. The idea of having someone else in my head is creepy."

After a pause, Saphira asked, "So, where do you want to set up camp? I think we can enjoy this lake one more day before we go to meet an uncertain future." Saphira and Elena smiled at each other.

"I know just the spot." Elena sat up and pointed to the southern edge of the lake. "Right there, by that little cluster of rocks. If you will get the fire started, then I'll take those hooks and catch us some fish to eat with our bread tonight."

Saphira squinted at the spot. "I'll try, but it will be a lot harder without any matches."

"Oh, don't worry about that. I have rocks."

"Great, but how will that help us?"

"Do you remember that night when Jillian bragged about making fire from rocks?"

"Yes."

"You just have to find the right ones: flint and magnesium. When you hit them together, they'll produce a spark." Elena got two gray stones out of her pocket and handed them to Saphira. "Here, I picked these up along the way."

Saphira turned them around in her hands. "Are these the flint or magnesium?"

Elena sighed. "The rock in your right hand is magnesium, and flint is in your left hand." She took the rocks back. "Watch." Elena struck their edges together. A spark jumped out and landed on the ground.

"That looks easy," Saphira said as Elena handed the stones back, "but somehow I sense that it will be harder than it looks to get that spark to go where I want it." Saphira put them in her pocket. "I'll gather the wood first. Hopefully you'll be done fishing by then so you can help me if I run across any problems."

Elena left, and Saphira gathered all the sticks she would need to make a tinder ball and feed the fire afterwards. Leaning over the small tufts of wood, she tried to replicate the spark Elena had made. She miscalculated and hit her fingers instead of the rocks several times before she was able to get a spark, and then when she got the spark, it didn't land where it was supposed to. She wished she had Elena or Jillian around to help her, but she kept trying. When she finally got a flame going, she shouted in joy.

Elena returned at dusk, and threw her fishing gear by the rest of their supplies.

"Do you like my fire?" Saphira asked.

Elena nodded. "I just wish I had something to add to it." She reached into the bag and pulled out a roll for her and Saphira.

As Saphira took the roll, she asked, "No luck?"

Elena shook her head. "Not one bite! I could see them, but they weren't interested in my bait. What kind of fish doesn't like worms?"

After dinner, they piled up the nearby moss and leaves to cushion their beds and fell asleep. Saphira slept soundly underneath her cloak, but Elena tossed and turned the entire night.

Elena was up early and went to the opposite side of the lake to take an official bath and try catching some fish to make up for her lack of success last night. The air was cool and the water felt warm getting in. After she was clean, she tried her line again. This time she squished some bread around the hook. Within five minutes, she had caught two big fish.

She quickly gutted them and couldn't keep the smile from her face as she headed back to camp. She was about to enter the path that led to their clearing when she heard noises and stopped. Sinking into the early morning shadows, she fell out of sight. She inched her way through the shrubbery, working her way towards the camp, trying to identify the sound.

Through a separation between some smaller trees, she saw gnomes going through the camp site. She covered her mouth and watched with huge eyes as they snuck up on Saphira's sleeping form. One of them was holding some rope. At a signal she didn't see, they all moved together to thrust the bedding aside, bind Saphira's arms and legs together, and shove fabric in her mouth to keep her from screaming.

Saphira was now awake and staring wide-eyed at the figures surrounding her. She shook and twisted her body to get away, but it was useless. She was completely subdued. A gnome made a circle with his finger, and the gnomes began to move around.

Elena shrank against the bush, out of sight, and didn't move again until the gnomes had returned to the main camp site. Elena used her finger to push aside some leaves and one eye watched as the gnomes picked Saphira up and headed south. A tear trickled down Elena's cheek, but she didn't move until they had been out of sight for several minutes.

She looked behind her, and then shook her head. "Not again," she whispered. She stood up slowly and cautiously walked around to the now deserted campsite. She placed her hand by a gnome track then looked to the south where they had exited. A small bush had two of its branches stripped of leaves. She walked over to it and noticed a small depression in the dirt underneath a plant not too far in front of her. "Thank you, Esau," she breathed out, as she moved towards it.

She followed the clues southwest until it led to a giant cave. There was a wide road leading up to it, with wagon ruts embedded into the rock before the entrance. Its front was guarded by several gnomes armed with swords and crossbows. She counted them and cursed silently to herself.

She backed up slowly and worked her way back to the campsite. She looked behind the rocks and sifted through the bedding that had been left behind. A sparkle caught her eye, and she picked out a jewel that had embedded itself in the moss. She put it in her hand and then reached down to find another one.

Staring down at the small fistful of jewels she was able to recover, she said, "I hope this will be enough." She then headed up the mountain to the Northern Cave.

Elena found the cave easily but hesitated at its entrance. It was too dark, too soon, and the air felt heavy and thick. Taking a deep breath, she took a few steps into the cave until she was completely surrounded by the darkness. She started to scream, but choked on the pitchy blackness and stumbled backwards. Tripping on a rock, she fell down, but she immediately flipped herself over and began crawling out of there as fast as she could. She curled up in a small patch of sun, away from the shadows, and tried to calm her breathing.

When it slowed, she forced herself to turn around and face the cave again.

She pushed herself to her knees and said, "Hello. Is anybody there? I want to talk to you. Can you tell me if this is the Northern Cave? I was told to meet someone here. If this isn't it, then I have a jewel you can have if you can just help me on my way." She took a gem out of her pocket and held it so that it sparkled in the sun.

"If you don't like that one, then you can have a different one. I have several to choose from." She removed some other jewels and placed them in her hand. She tilted them so that they faced the entrance to the cave.

"Who are you?"

Elena jumped. It was the same disembodied voice she and Saphira had heard earlier but this time it was accompanied by a pair of bright yellow eyes that stared at her from the darkness of the cave.

"My name is Elena."

"Are you the one who carries the shakra?"

"No, but if you could help me anyway..."

"Where is your companion?" the voice asked quickly.

"She was captured by gnomes this morning."

"How could you let that happen?" the voice shouted. "Where did they take her?"

"I followed her to the mine entrance. They must have gone inside."

"And they took the shakra with them?" the voice demanded, not asking.

"No. We never had the shakra. You must have been mistaken, but if you would..."

"I was not mistaken!" The voice cut her off. "Come inside. I have to know everything."

The eyes disappeared, and the sound of padded feet faded deeper into the cave. Elena swallowed hard before stepping back into the darkness. Again, it wrapped around her body, urging her to stop. She hesitated, and the voice asked angrily, "Are you coming?"

"I...I can't see."

"No, of course not. You have to come inside before you can do that."

Elena bit her bottom lip and slowly inched her way deeper into the interior of the cave. It just got darker. Elena closed her eyes and forced herself to take several more steps. Suddenly the darkness ended, and she opened her eyes in surprise.

She was in the middle of a bright, airy room. It was empty of any kind of furnishings, but there were other doors and openings off the main chamber that led deeper into the cave.

The only other thing in the room, besides herself, was the creature. From far away, it might have looked like a human. It was tall and lean with light tan skin and dark brown hair that was longer than current fashion trends. The skin however, was both human and reptilian. His face was smooth, but his arms were scaled with a faint diamond pattern traveling up the inside his arm. His pupils were also yellow, although smaller, and not as shocking as she remembered.

"What happened to the shakra?" the creature demanded.

"We never had it. We just had some shiny gems. Saphira's diviner helped her think of solutions to problems, but it wasn't magical, and it certainly wasn't the mythical weapon."

"Fool. It was more powerful than you can imagine. That 'diviner' *gave* her the answers to her questions and could have easily defeated the gnomes in the right hands. How could you humans have forgotten what shakras looked like?"

Elena's head lowered.

The creature breathed heavily down the back of his throat, and Elena backed away from him. "Stay here while I search the grounds and do not touch anything. Let us hope the shakra fell somewhere the gnomes didn't see. *Their* minds have not been as forgetful."

Elena watched as he spread his arms out away from his body. They continued to move past his shoulder blades, growing thinner and wider as they traveled across his back. He bent over as thick, broad legs grew from his chest to match his back legs which had also thickened. His skin turned green as his neck grew longer, and a tail began to form at the base of his spine. Ridges formed along his joints, and a giant scaled beast in grand dragon tradition now stood before her.

His claws scratched, making clicking sounds on the floor as he worked his way towards the dark hole. The opening was clearly too small for him to fit through, but Elena watched with amazement as the entrance changed size. The frame followed the contours of the dragon's body until it returned to its original size. The last thing Elena saw was the dragon's tail swishing lightly side to side as it disappeared into the darkness.

It seemed like hours before Elena saw the dragon's head reappear. The same miraculous feats with the cave entrance and the transformation process were repeated in reverse. The person-ish form turned to face Elena. "It is bad."

"What happened? What did you find out?"

"The shakra is not outside. Either your companion has it, or it was taken by a gnome. I searched for her presence near the mines, but I couldn't find her. They must have taken her deeper into the mountains, beyond my range. I fear they are taking her to Trevastan, and if they are, then your friend is lost. The king will take her shakra and then destroy her."

"Then we must stop him," Elena said, clenching her fist.

"It's too late," he said, shaking his head. "They are too far ahead of us. We could never catch them in time."

"So you're going to do....nothing?"

"No, I am going to take you to the elves. Once the gnomes discover you saw a shakra, they will come after you. The elves can protect you better. They don't normally allow outsiders among them, but they'll make an exception for me."

"I can't believe a dragon could be so, so spiritless."

"How do you think I survived all these years? It is those 'spirited' dragons that rushed headlong into traps and didn't think about the consequences of their actions until it was too late."

"Fine. You hide, but I'm going after Saphira. I am not going to run away. I didn't come all this way to give up on everyone I ever loved just because things look bad." Elena was stomping towards the entrance when he reached out an arm and held her back.

"Where do you think you are going?"

She turned to face him. "To the mines, and then Trevastan if I can."

"And just how are you planning to get there? They have sensors all along the entrance that notify them if anyone crosses into their territory. You would be caught before you got a hundred feet."

"Then I'll sneak in with the next caravan or wagon that goes in." She tried again to get past him, but his grip was too strong.

"Stop." The dragon sighed. "I still think you would be wiser to forget them and think about your own preservation, but if you are going to insist on going, then I can show you a less guarded way to get there. It will not be pleasant, but it will take you directly to Trevastan."

Elena stopped struggling. "Why didn't you mention this earlier?"

"Because, it will only help you get past their initial guard. You still will not succeed. You will be captured and end your days in one of their pits. I think you are being reckless and foolhardy, and the most you will do is shock them by proving that their entrance warning systems can somehow be bypassed."

"I'm willing to take that chance. Lead me on to the biggest shock of their gnome lives."

Reunion

Saphira was in a nightmare. The arms that held her were like iron, and she couldn't shake them loose. She was slung over a shoulder and could only stare in horror as the ground changed from the small rocks and sand of the lake shore to the wooded paths of the forest to the smooth gray floor of the caves. They traveled for hours, always going deeper and deeper into the mountain. She was frightened, growing stiff, and contemplating all the bruises that would be forming tomorrow.

She was getting used to the swaying motion of their quiet running when a door suddenly shut behind her. She was surprised to see it and wondered what they had just entered. She tried to move her head to examine her surroundings more carefully. They were still traveling fast, but slowed down as they entered a large open enclosure. Other gnomes stopped and stared at her party as they sped by. She was taken through several other doors before they finally came to a stop.

They repositioned her body so she looked like a baby nestled against its parent's chests. The sudden change made her woozy, but she soon regained her equilibrium. She looked around as the gnomes carried her forward, further into a giant receiving room of some sort. There were several alcoves on its sides, and huge red banners emblazoned with golden names hung from the ceiling. They walked forward towards a magnificently carved, raised throne.

The gnomes took her to the front of the throne's dais. They placed her gently on the floor and allowed her to stand. Unfortunately, her muscles were stiff. When she tried to balance herself, the bindings on her legs caught her, and she fell over.

A magnificently dressed creature jumped off the throne and landed at her side. It had a small golden crown and long, fur lined robes. She tried to wiggle away until she saw its face.

"Impossible," she breathed out as her urge to flee disappeared. It was Jack! He bent over her and gently caressed her face. She blushed under his touch. He faced the gnomes again and yelled at them so harshly she couldn't understand a word he said. They backed away, Jack glaring at them until the door shut behind them.

Once they had left, Jack gently untied the cords and massaged the areas that had turned red. He had several harsh things to say about the gnomes and asked her if anything hurt or if she needed anything as he worked the soreness out of her body. All she could think was, *This isn't real. It can't be happening.*

"Jack?" she finally asked.

"In the flesh."

"But, I thought..."

"I was a prisoner? I was. But as you can see, things have changed since then."

"How?"

Jack sat down next to Saphira. "As you know we came down here to trade with the gnomes. Everything was going as expected until a gnome recognized us from our earlier incident with them. He had been injured when Charlemane went after the money. He told the king, and our trading came to a halt. We were sent to the mines, and our goods were confiscated. I might have been there still if I hadn't found a way to help the king.

"Not everyone here is loyal to him or his policies. There are some gnomes whose views are so anti-human that they refuse to see any reason on a topic that includes us. At the best, they believe we should be enslaved and treated like pack animals. At worst, they believe we should be treated like cave snakes and killed on sight. There are many guards who watch over us in the mines who share that last view and are only restrained by the fact that they would lose their positions if they followed through with their desires.

"While I was working, I overheard some of them make plans to get rid of their king and place someone more sympathetic to their views in his place. I was able to warn him, and he rewarded me generously. I became his top advisor, and as I proved myself, I earned the role of successor. As soon as that happened, I sent for you."

"You sent for me?" Saphira said as her heart did a flip. "Why would you send for me?"

"Because I can't imagine life without you," Jack told her, and Saphira had to remind herself to keep breathing. He stroked her cheek tenderly. "Saphira, you are my world, and now I can give you everything you deserve. We never have to be apart again."

"Oh, Jack." She didn't have time to say anymore before he was kissing her, smothering any words she might have said.

When he finished, she pulled back and touched his face with her hand. "I always knew you were alive. But I never saw any letters after you entered. When did you write for me?"

"I didn't write. I thought a personal escort would be more fitting."

"A personal escort? Who did you send?"

"Gnomes, of course."

Saphira suddenly remembered the gnomes who had "visited." "Jack, you should never have done that. Those gnomes…you won't believe what they did to the town."

Jack smiled. "They did tell me they were 'enthusiastic' in their search for you."

"Enthusiastic? They burned it to the ground! They killed people! Our people!" Saphira tried to stand but lost her balance and fell.

Jack immediately went to help her. He picked her up and placed her in his throne. "Shh. It's all right," he said, stroking the side of her cheek. "The gnomes were just trying too hard. I told them not to leave without you, and when you weren't immediately produced, they thought you were being held captive.

"When the gnomes returned from Hallenbreth, I couldn't understand why you were not with them. And when they said there had been casualties...." Jack turned his head and stared at the ground. "If they had just brought everyone here, I could have talked to them. I could have gotten some hint as to where you had gone. And when I thought that one of the losses might have accidentally been you..." His fingers stilled and began to dig into her skin. "No punishment seemed severe enough for them."

"Ow," Saphira called out, and Jack quickly released his grip. Saphira rubbed the area where his hands had been. "They made a mistake. A horrible, awful mistake, but you can't blame yourself for it."

"I did then, and when I didn't see your parents among the survivors..."

Saphira interrupted Jack, "My parents?"

Jack shook his head. "I'm sorry. They had been particularly forceful with them."

"No!" Saphira tried to stand, but Jack forced her to sit back down again. She looked up at him with tears streaming down her face. "They can't be..." She shook her head, but in her heart she knew they were dead. She dropped her head. All the hope she had carried died as sobs racked her body. He scooped her up and carried her around the back of the dais as if she weighed no more than a newborn. She saw a door shut behind them, as she was carried down a long hallway.

After a hundred yards, her tears had quieted enough for her to hear Jack talking again. He was talking quietly into her ear. "You can stay here as long as you like. The west suite rooms will be perfect for you. I will send some servants to look after you once you've had some time to calm down, but I don't want you to worry. They won't harm you in any way. If they so much as look at you in a way you don't like, then let me know, and I will have them removed immediately."

He put her down in front of a door. When he opened it, Saphira was stunned at what she saw. The room would have been grand on any scale. There was a large comfortable canopy bed in the center of the far wall, with a sitting area on the right. On the left there was a desk filled with papers, ink, and pencils. But most amazing of all were a series of five windows set into her wall. She stumbled over to them and tried to open one so the wind could dry the tears from her face, but it came off the wall and fell to the floor. Behind it was a solid wall. She looked back at what she realized now was a picture.

"Careful," Jack said, picking up the, thankfully, unbroken picture and placing it back on the wall. "Everything in here is built to last, but it is not unbreakable."

Saphira glanced back at the picture and said, "How did they do that? It looked so real."

Jack smiled. "I told you they were good. Tapestries are another of their skills."

Saphira looked at the pictures more closely, surprise stopping the tears. The wooden frames held pictures of green fields that reminded her of home. Some showed crop fields while others were open pastures for cows and horses. One tapestry showed a small farm with a young girl tending to some pigs in the forefront while a young man was calming a bucking horse in the background. Then she realized that these weren't humans. Gnomes were doing these chores.

She turned around when she heard Jack speaking. "You should be able to find everything you need easily, but if something is missing, you have but to ask, and someone will bring it to you."

Saphira shook her head. "This is all too much."

"Nonsense. It's time you got used to such treatment." Jack tilted her chin up and kissed her. "I wish I could stay, but I promised the king I'd tell him as soon as you arrived. I'm sure he will want to meet you as soon as you are ready."

"The king? But…" Saphira looked at the floor. She wasn't ready to meet anyone else yet.

"Don't worry," Jack said, "You just need some time to rest. By tomorrow, you'll feel a lot better. I have you safe now, and I promise that I will never let you go again."

He squeezed her hand, and a tiny glow begin to spread through her body. She may have lost her parents, but at least she still had Jack. By the time he left, she felt good enough to explore her new room. Her fingers touched everything as she walked from one wall to the other side. The quilted covers were thick and soft, the wooden furniture highly-polished and smooth to the touch, and the drawers opened and shut noiselessly. The colored sheets of paper inside slid easily against each other and were her mother's favorite shade of pink. She quickly shifted her gaze to the ceiling. She was blinking rapidly when she heard a soft tap on the door.

She opened the door to see a stout, elderly gnome woman. Her hair was piled on top of her head, and around her neck was a string of beads holding a two-toned glass rimmed monocle and a cloth ruler. Behind her was a younger female whose arms were overflowing with cloths and ribbons. Some pencils were sticking out of her bun. They both curtseyed, and Saphira was amazed the assistant could keep everything in her arms upright while she did that.

When she stood back up, the older lady looked Saphira over as she said, "I'm pleased to meet you, my lady. My name is Annabelle, and I will be your new seamstress. I was told to complete some dresses for you as soon as possible. If you will stand straight right over here," she said, indicating an open section of the room, "then we can begin."

Saphira moved over, and Annabelle, very efficiently, began taking measurements. She only talked to Saphira when she wanted her to change position. As she moved the ruler around, Annabelle gave a constant stream of words and numbers to her assistant: "Left Arm: 24, Right arm: 23 ¾ Waist: 30. Underarm to waist: 10, Waist to floor: 36" and so on until she was done.

"We can go ahead and get started with these measurements. We'll make the final adjustments on the dresses tomorrow. You don't have a bad form, for a human, and in the right clothes, you will look magnificent. Until we can get those ready for you, I have a dress that we'll be able to make work for you back at the shop. At the very least it will be clean." She looked down at Saphira's clothes as if to emphasize her point.

Saphira was confused. "But…don't you want my opinion on anything: color, style, accessories?"

Annabelle laughed. "My lady, you haven't had one of my dresses. I have an eye for this kind of thing. It's why I was chosen. Trust me, you will look magnificent." Annabelle curtseyed one last time before leaving. Her assistant followed behind her.

Saphira didn't have to wait long before she heard another knock and opened the door to reveal a gnome maid holding a fluffy, towel-like robe draped over one arm and a platter with the other hand. On the tray was soap and a bowl containing a thick liquid substance she didn't recognize but smelled wonderful. The maid curtseyed deeply before coming inside.

"If you please, my lady, I'm to be your new abigail."

Saphira nodded. "What's your name?"

"It's Rapella, my lady."

"What's in your arms?" Saphira pointed to the tray.

"I heard that you would be wanting to clean up after your trip here, so I brought you some supplies."

Suddenly Saphira's clothes started to itch. "That would be lovely. Where can I go to freshen up?"

Rapella smiled. "Just follow me." She headed towards the bed, turned right at the sitting area, and then continued straight through the wall. Saphira was shocked as the stones rippled away from Rapella's body as she passed.

She inched closer and called out, "Rapella?"

"Yes, ma'am?" Rapella replied in a muted voice.

"Humans can't walk through walls."

Rapella laughed. The wall spread apart as Rapella stepped back into the room. "Neither can we. Come." She waved Saphira closer.

When Saphira was a foot away Rapella shook the walls and Saphira groaned. "I feel so stupid. I never thought you could get a curtain to match the walls so perfectly. This is the second time I've been tricked. It's obvious you have some amazing skills with fabrics."

"Thank you. We are rather proud of our work." Rapella re-entered the washroom and Saphira followed her. The fabric closed quietly behind them.

The washroom made her feel like she was underwater. A giant mirror lined one wall, and the rest of the room was painted, or woven, blue with murals of coral and fish on them. A dressing table with a padded chair faced the mirror and a giant pedestal tub lay in the middle of the room. Behind it was a lever that Rapella pulled. Water came rushing down from the ceiling and landed in the tub until Rapella let go. As the steam filled the room, Saphira sensed what a fish felt like. It wasn't unpleasant.

"Do you always put so much detail into your rooms?"

"Here we do. You're in one of the royal guest rooms, and one might say that this whole area is a tribute to gnome artistry. Everything in here was designed and built by our best craftsmen. I can't remember how many artists over the years have been called to work on one thing or another."

Rapella stirred the bath water again. This time she was pleased with the temperature. "Are you ready to get in, my lady?"

"Yes. But if you don't mind, I would like to bathe myself. I think I recognize the soap, and I'll call you when I want help with my hair."

"You don't have to worry about my wishes. It's me that's here to serve you to the extent you want me. I'll just wait on the other side of the curtain so I can help you as soon as you are ready for me."

Rapella withdrew and pulled the curtain closed behind her. Saphira took off her clothes and placed them in a pile in the corner. From around her neck, she removed the small pouch she had made for her diviner. She looked at it, and then brought it over towards the tub with her. She dumped it out into her hand and rinsed it in the warm water. When it was clean, she dried it off, and set it in the middle of a towel. She then got in the tub herself. She sighed in joy as the warm water covered her shoulders. She plugged her nose, and let it cover her face.

She had thought the lake had been wonderful, but it couldn't compare to a heated bath. She sat back up and wiped the water off her face. She then washed everything but her hair. The soap was soft and fragrant and took off dirt that Saphira had given up hope of removing. She felt a little bit better with each body part that she cleaned.

After she was done soaking, she dried off and wrapped the bathrobe around her body. She then grabbed the diviner and placed it in her pocket. She wasn't ready for Rapella to ask her questions about it yet, because she knew she would have to talk about her parents if she did, and she had done enough crying for the day. She poked her head around the curtain and called, "Rapella?"

Rapella was sitting in the chair by the desk, and said, "Yes, miss."

"Can you help me with my hair, now?"

Rapella smiled. "Of course, my lady." She immediately followed her back into the bathroom and directed Saphira to sit in the chair she had pulled behind her to the tub. Saphira sat down, and Rapella leaned it back against the side of the tub. The top of the chair was curved down at the top so Saphira has a comfortable resting place for her head. She almost fell asleep as Rapella rubbed one of the unknown liquids into her hair. It smelled sweet, and the rhythmic motion of Rapella's fingers circling the soap into a lather was a luxurious sensation.

She bit her lip to keep herself from begging Rapella to wash her hair again when it was time for the final rinse. Rapella towel-dried Saphira's hair before getting a comb out of the vanity drawer. Gently, she picked all the knots out of Saphira's hair. It was a long task, but when she finished, Saphira's hair lay smooth and flat against her scalp. Its glorious yellow color had returned.

Rapella pulled out a pair of scissors and asked permission to trim Saphira's hair.

Saphira laughed. "I think my hair needs something more than a trim." She played with some strands between her fingers and thought about Jack. "I think it's time for something a little more flattering."

Rapella smiled. "I know just what to do."

When she was done, Saphira couldn't stop playing with her hair. It was a lot shorter than she was used to, but its soft curls and the way it seemed to float around her head made her feel surprisingly feminine.

"You're a genius," Saphira said in awe.

"I'm glad you like it," Rapella said proudly before she helped Saphira into the gown the sewing assistant had brought over.

"Your dinner will arrive shortly. You've had a long day and Lord Kinyard thought you would enjoy a quiet dinner in your room tonight."

"Lord Kinyard? Oh, you mean Jack."

"Yes, my lady." After a pause she asked, "Is there anything else I can do for you?"

"Yes, can you tell me when I will get to see 'Lord Kinyard' again?"

"He's a busy man, but I have no doubt he'll find a way to see you tomorrow morning at the latest." Rapella smiled, and Saphira couldn't keep an answering smile from her own face.

Just then there was a knock on the door. Rapella opened it to let in a wheeled cart carrying a dome-covered silver platter. Rapella directed the servant to place the cart by the bed before she took her leave. "If you need anything, then just pull the blue tassel by your bed. Someone will come in immediately to help you." Saphira thanked her before turning her attention to her dish.

Saphira lifted the lid and its aromas were fully released for the first time. The dish held one of her favorite meals, the one she always picked as her birthday request. It smelled so much like home, she cried. She was suddenly glad Jack wasn't there. A quiet meal was just what she needed. Too many things had happened at once. She needed some time to process them.

When Jack knocked on her door the next day, Saphira opened it, wearing Annabelle's latest creation, a light-blue gown made out of a material Saphira couldn't name. "You're finally here. I thought you'd never come." She threw her arms around him and held tight.

Jack laughed at her as he moved her just enough so he could enter. "Why the anxiety? Weren't the gnomes kind to you?"

"Yes, but it's not the same. I needed *you*."

Jack's face softened and he bent down to kiss her gently on the lips. "You have me now," he promised. He then held her back so he could get a good look at her. She got a better look at him, too. He was wearing a dark blue coat trimmed with aged yellow lacing and black pantaloons. She wondered if he had known what she was going to wear, and had chosen his outfit to match.

Jack reached a hand out to her hair and followed its curve back to her cheek. "I love what you did with your hair."

Saphira blushed. "It was all Rapella's idea. I would never have thought of this on my own. And the dress maker you sent was amazing. When I walk, the movement is so free and fluid I feel like nothing can drag me down for long."

Jack took her hand and squeezed it gently. "I couldn't have asked for them to do a better job then. "Now tell me, my love. Are you ready to meet King Brackster?"

Saphira startled. "Already?"

Jack nodded. "I told you he'd be anxious to meet you."

"But, I have no idea what I should say to him."

"You don't have to say anything, my love. You look beautiful."

Saphira made a scoffing noise before allowing him to escort her back into the hallway. As they walked, Jack asked about how she had gotten to the mountainside in the first place.

"I had left Hallenbreth thinking I could come down here and rescue you." Saphira laughed. "Elena joined me and..."

"Elena?" Jack stopped walking. "She was with you?"

Spahira stopped, too. "Didn't your gnomes find her at the same time they found me?" Saphira's quickly covered her mouth and her eyes widened. "You don't think the gnomes thought she was holding me captive and, and ...."

"No, no, no." Jack took her hand down. "They learned their lesson the last time. They would never have killed one of your traveling companions. Where did you see her last?"

"She was by the lake." Saphira bit her bottom lip. "What if something happened to her?"

"I doubt that." He spotted a servant walking past them and called him over. "Silen, find Gorlock and have him assemble a small search party to find a lady who is still wandering around our mountains. Her name is Elena and she will probably be disguised as a boy." He looked towards Saphira who nodded.

"Tell him to begin his search at the lake where Saphira was found, and tell him to be more thorough in his search than the last group was. We don't want her having to spend another night away from her friend."

Silen clapped his left hand to his side and left.

"Do you think they will find her? Maybe we should have given them a better description."

"You don't need to. Gorlock is our best hunter. Nothing can hide from him for long."

Saphira managed to smile. "Thank you. I can't imagine what happened to her, or what she would think if she returned to camp. It would have looked bad."

"Don't worry about her anymore. You will be reunited with her tomorrow, I promise."

"That would be wonderful." She smiled up at Jack who lifted the edges of his own mouth in response.

"Speaking of wonderful, when do you want to have the wedding?" Jack asked as they resumed walking.

"Whenever people can arrive. I want to share my joy with as many people as possible." Saphira's voice grew softer. "I wish my parents could have seen this. You and all you've become. They would have been so proud to give me away." Saphira sniffed back a tear, "But they can't, and I knew when I left home, that there was a chance I would never see them again. I just never thought…."

"I know. But the sooner I can make you mine, the sooner I can fill all your days and nights with happiness."

Saphira blushed as Jack continued, "A month would be enough time to plan a wedding, don't you think?"

Saphira laughed. "A month? You have got to be joking."

"Why not? I can't think of anyone outside these mountains I care enough to delay the wedding for. We can send emissaries to publish the news of our betrothal tomorrow."

"No, that would not be nearly enough time to plan everything."

"Make it two then, but I don't want to wait any longer than that."

Jack stopped and wrapped his arms around Saphira. He pulled her in closer for a kiss, but before he could deliver it, Saphira teased, "You are so impatient."

"I am not," he growled gently. "I have waited a lifetime for you. Isn't that long enough?"

Saphira laughed, but it faded away as his head dropped and his lips joined hers.

Jack eventually finished escorting her to a side room. It looked like they had stepped outside, but Saphira was not going to be fooled a third time. The air was too cool and they were too deep for that to be true, but the animals didn't seem to mind. They all looked healthy, but she must have surprised them because they had all stopped what they were doing to stare at her. A bunny neglected his clover, a frog halted mid spring, and birds cocked their heads towards her from their places in the tress. She felt unnerved, waiting for something to happen. Why weren't they moving, talking…anything?

She hit her head with her palm. They had tricked her *again*. "How did the gnomes do this? They are so lifelike. Are they stuffed?"

"No. This is just some more of the gnomeadic artistry I once told you about. They created everything in here: the animals, the plants, even the sky. It's incredible isn't it?"

"That's an understatement." Saphira took several more steps into the room. She reached out to touch one of the animals when Jack stopped her.

"Wait. Put these on first. Oils in our skin can ruin the pieces if we are not careful." Jack handed her a pair of gloves, and Saphira slipped them on. The glove material was soft, and it stretched to fit her hand perfectly.

She stroked the side of the horse, and she thought she could feel its muscles quivering under her touch. She proceeded around the rest of the room. She patted the rough bark of a tree, caressed the soft petals of a flower, and almost ran into the wall, not realizing until the last second that it was painted and not an extension of the room.

"How did they get everything so…perfect?" Saphira asked.

"Practice."

Saphira jumped when the answering voice did not belong to Jack. An old gnome stood up so she could now see him from behind a bush. He waved his cane towards the exhibit. "It's amazing what you can get done with a little time and patience. Every known material and technique was tested until our artists created the perfect copy of an animal hair or eye. This room holds several of their masterpieces."

"Your Majesty," Jack said and bowed deeply. Saphira looked at the gnome again. So this was the king. "Your Majesty," she stumbled after Jack. She started to bow when she realized she was a girl again and changed it into a curtsey. When she rose, King Brackster was looking at her oddly, and she wondered if she had done something wrong. What had Jillian said about proper gnome etiquette? Had Jack mentioned anything in his letters? She was just about to run when King Brackster spoke again.

"You *are* a lovely creature. I thought Jack was exaggerating when he described you to me, but I now see that he doesn't know enough words to do you justice." King Brackster smiled at her, and Saphira began to relax. He seemed so calm and reasonable. If he had been at her town, then he would not have allowed the violence to take place. She could see why Jack respected him so much. "Thank you, your majesty. At least Jack knows enough words to have gained your favor. I never expected to meet him again as someone so important to your retinue."

"I wasn't expecting it either, when I first met him. I didn't think it would be possible to find someone of his character among the humans, but he proved me wrong. When you find someone like Jack, you just can't let them go."

Saphira squeezed Jack's hand and smiled up at him. Maybe, between the two of them, they could change all the gnome's negative feelings towards humans. "I understand how you feel. He is not the kind of man that is easy to replace." Jack stood a little straighter.

"But what about you?" King Brackster questioned. "Would you be willing to work with the gnomes as he has?"

Saphira thought of her parents and how meaningless their deaths had been. "Your Majesty, I am willing to work with anyone or anything to promote peace and prosperity. Our species are not so different that I don't think we can find a way to make that happen if everyone is as reasonable as you are."

King Brackster smiled at that. "That, my dear, was the perfect answer. I think Jack has chosen very well for himself."

The king moved towards the door, leaning only slightly on his cane. As he opened the door, he said, "I will leave you two love birds now to coo all you want in peace. The grand ballroom shall be at your disposal for the wedding."

"Thank you, your majesty." Jack said, and the door closed behind the king, leaving them alone again.

Jack and Saphira spent the rest of the day talking together as they had in the days before Jack set out on his trip. She could almost pretend that nothing had changed.

Changes

The next day, Saphira received the rest of her dresses and put on the orange one because Rapella told her that color was considered lucky in their culture. It had soft yellow flowers with gauze petals detailed into the skirting and a wide, matching yellow sash that began just under her bodice. She asked Rapella where she might find Jack and went to see if he had heard any news about Elena. From the other side of the throne room doors, she could make out angry voices. Actually, it was just one angry voice, and it was Jack's. She was about to retreat when she heard Elena's name. She pressed her ear against the door.

"What do you mean you can't find her? I gave you a complete description and last known location. She can't have vanished into thin air."

"Forgive us," a quivering voice replied. "Looking again and backtracking their trail, we did find indications that there were two traveling companions, but after the lake, nothing."

"So you're going to try and make me believe an animal got her?" Jack sneered. Saphira had never heard such a tone come out of him before. It was mocking and dismissive and…evil. This was nothing like the Jack she knew and interacted with. She shivered.

"You and I both know," Jack continued, "that there is nothing in these woods that could cause someone to just disappear. She has to be around here somewhere. Did you check the village again? Did you question the townspeople? She might have gone there to try and get help when she realized Saphira was gone."

"My lord, we did go to the nearest town and visited several other villages within a ten mile radius, but no one remembered seeing anyone coming out of the mountains."

"Did you question them thoroughly?"

"Yes."

"Are you sure you used every method at your disposal to extract information?"

"Yes, my lord. They knew nothing."

"So what did you do next?"

"We came back to tell you the news."

"That's it? That's all you have to say to me. This is unacceptable. I gave you a simple order, and you failed me. After you searched a few houses, you decided, what? That the search was impossible and gave up. What would have happened if Thornad had stopped fighting the Legon? What would have happened if Eplore refused to go beyond the next rise? Where would your great civilization be now if others gave up as readily as you?" Jack's voice turned dangerously quiet. "I am beyond disappointed in you."

"Well, there is one possibility about what happened to her that would explain her disappearance, and why we can't find her."

"And what is that?" Jack mocked.

"We think it might be possible that she came across a dragon." Saphira gasped, but Jack didn't even pause at that suggestion.

"A dragon? You are stupider than I thought. I can't believe you think they can still exist. All the dragons that might have existed are dead and have been dead for centuries."

"But the wolves still stay away from our hills. They are everywhere else. There is no reason for them not to be here unless there is a greater predator they sense."

"Then the predator is us." Saphira could practically hear Jack's teeth snapping together. He continued, "Go back out there and don't come back until you find her."

Saphira didn't want to hear anymore. She turned around and ran back up the hallway. What had made Jack so mean? He was downright vile. She didn't know that person. When had he changed? She found herself in front of the room with the animals and entered.

She needed time to think about what she had just heard. She couldn't understand where Jack was coming from. Had she lost her connection with him already? No, impossible. He was her Jack and would always be her Jack. He wasn't really the snarling creature she pictured on the other side of the door. It must be stress. Poor, Jack. She was determined to do what she could to help him. As she thought about how she could broach the subject and ways she might be able to help him, Jack entered the room. He was wearing a big smile, with no sign of frustration in his bearing.

"There you are," Jack said, coming up to her. "I was beginning to worry I would never find you."

"I'm sorry, I should have left a note, but I didn't decide to come here until the last minute." A deer stood on Saphira's left side, and her hand began playing with its hair. "I have to confess that I overheard you talking in the throne room." She stopped touching the deer and faced Jack. "You sounded stressed. Is there anything I could do to help?"

"That's nice, but you don't need to worry your pretty little head about that." Jack ran his fingers through her hair. "I was just upset because your friend is still out there somewhere. I guess my worry for her got ahead of me. I'm sorry we haven't found her yet."

"Did the gnomes have any ideas what might have happened to her?"

Jack laughed and waved his hand dismissively. "Whenever someone disappears, they always say 'a dragon got them.' It has no meaning."

"So you don't think dragons really exist? We met a lady in the last town we visited who believed that they did."

"I'm not surprised. There are lots of people who also believe in leprechauns, imps, and starlings. Do all those exist as well?" he asked, an eyebrow rising.

"I...I..."

"Of course not." Jack spoke with such conviction that Saphira laughed at herself and Elena for thinking they might have been heading to a dragon's lair. She smoothed the deer's hairs back down. *But that voice?* If it wasn't a dragon, then what sent it…and the vision.? What would they have found if they actually made it to the cave? She paused. "Jack," she asked, "is it possible they missed a place during their search?"

Jack snorted. "They obviously did, but is there a particular location you had in mind?"

"Yes." Saphira took a deep breath. "There's a cave, close to where the gnomes found me called the Northern Cave."

"What about it?"

"There was a lady in town that happened to mention it. She and some friends liked to play near it when they were younger. We had been planning to head there the day I was captured. We thought it would provide some shelter while we figured out a way in to rescue you." She couldn't quite bring herself to mention the person, or thing, they hoped to meet there. Jack's brows came together like they always did when he concentrated. Suddenly they broke apart, and he started laughing.

"That would explain it then. That place has a reputation as a dragon cave. If she did go in there, then there's no way the gnomes would have gone in after her. They're scared of the place although there's no reason for it. Write a note for her, and the gnomes will deliver it tomorrow. You can let her know that she has nothing to fear from the gnomes. If she will go to the mine entrance, then you two can be reunited shortly."

"I will do that right now," Saphira said. She kissed his cheek quickly before leaving to write her letter. Sitting in front of her desk, she bit the end of her quill several times as she wrote and then rewrote the beginning of the letter. She finally settled on the following:

Elena,
    You will never believe what has happened. I have found Jack, and it is completely different from what we were expecting. I wish you were here so I could talk to you again and let you know everything that has happened because it's impossible to put it all down on paper.
    Your Dearest Friend,
    Saphira

She copied it onto a sheet of light blue paper, and blew on it gently to dry the ink. She remembered the last note she wrote and had to stop. Her last letter had been filled with such hope. Now, she was with Jack again, but it wasn't the pure joy she had been expecting. She shook her head and sealed the letter. Just then, there was a knock at the door, shortly followed by Jack.

"Is that the letter for Elena?" he asked

Saphira nodded. "I just finished it."

"I have perfect timing then. I'll place it with my note and have it delivered immediately." He held out his hand for the letter. Saphira knew a moment of hesitation before she handed it to Jack.

Don't be silly, she scolded herself. *There's no reason you can't trust Jack with your mail. What do you think he's going to do with it anyway?* She handed it to him, and he put it in an inside vest pocket.

"As an apology for not getting Elena for you, I have arranged a meeting tomorrow with several of our old acquaintances. Your neighbors are very excited to see you again."

Saphira squealed and gave Jack a big hug. "I can hardly wait. I had wondered where they had gone. What happened after they arrived?"

"I offered to let them stay or return home. I compensated them for the loss of their homes, and most of them opted to start a new life here. Some will be too busy tomorrow to come, but the rest will join us for lunch. Meanwhile, I thought you might enjoy seeing gnomes create some of those things you've been admiring. It's a fascinating process."

"I would love that. Will they be weaving, making animals, or painting?"

"They, my dear, will be making a sculpture. I commissioned it months ago, the same time that I sent for you. They've been working on it ever since, and it's almost done. I would like to get your opinion on it."

Jack took her arm, and together they walked to the throne room. He led her down a new corridor that began with some very pretty murals that gradually faded away until the walls were just smooth tunnels of solid gray. When she looked up she would occasionally see a small fixture, the same color of the walls, shedding light on the passageway through small designs that had been carved into the lamp. She had never noticed them before.

"Why is this part of the castle so plain?" Saphira asked.

"It's just newer. The king wanted to connect the artists' studios directly to his castle so he had this built. Soon, it will look exactly like the rest of the castle."

She pointed to the ceiling, "What's in those lamps? They look like they would be hard to refill."

He looked up. "They are, but they're filled with very special oil that can remain lit for an entire year as long as it doesn't come into contact with any wood."

"What happens if it does?"

Jack laughed. "Then you had better stand back."

Saphira remembered the aftermath of the gnome's fire on her town and fell silent. If Jack had seen it, too, then he wouldn't have laughed either.

They continued on their way until they reached a heavy wooden door. When he opened it, a pleasant warmth brushed against her skin in the cool hallway. He ushered her inside, and she stopped to stare at…herself.

She had been transformed into a giant carving. As she looked around, she realized it wasn't the only statue in the room, but it was certainly the largest. Four gnomes surrounded her double and debated what should be added next. They all bore the mark of their trade: spots of dye and scorch marks covered their clothes and faces. They stopped their work and bowed off to the sides of the room when they saw Jack.

Saphira walked slowly up to the statue. She couldn't help comparing herself to it. The lines of the body, the coloring of the skin, eyes, and hair – it was perfect. How could they have captured her so exactly?

She was wearing the outfit she had worn to her coming out party a lifetime ago. They had even put the blue flowers in her hair, her father's flowers. She smiled. He would always be a part of her. They had positioned her arms and legs to mimic Rhonda's. She had struck that pose too many times not to recognize it now. After Jack's letter about her, she had pretended she was Rhonda and Jack was the moon god coming to take her away.

"Do you like it?" Jack asked as he came up to stand beside her.

"I don't know what to say. It's beautiful."

"When they are done with you, they will begin one of me. When I thought I had lost you, I spent hours down here helping them perfect every little detail. I didn't want the world to ever forget that you existed. They did a good job, but nothing can compare to the original."

Jack pointed to the various features of the statue as he talked about them. "We had to look at 200 different Sapphires before we found the perfect match for your eyes. As for your hair, well, that was its own challenge. Do you know how many different shades of yellow your hair holds?

"We made new gold alloys and covered them with dozens of dye combinations until we found the perfect matches. I can't remember how much iodine and turmeric we had to go through and as for the onions, well, even my eyes started to water when I entered the dye room. Luckily, we were able to get more from some local farmers when our original supplies began to run low. It was quite a task. I think they are working on a batch of gold for another one of their projects. Do you want to see the process?"

"Yes, I do."

Jack led her further into the room and opened a second door. A wave of heat instantly washed over her. It was like sharing the room with the sun, and she began dripping sweat immediately. The cause was easily identifiable. In the center of the room there was an open pit where red hot liquid oozed past. It didn't affect the cauldrons, but melted everything else in the room, including Saphira.

"That red liquid is called lava. It's the hottest thing in the world," Jack explained.

"It's incredible. I can't believe something so intense could be found somewhere so naturally cold."

Jack smiled as he looked at it. "This is the real secret behind our metal working success. We can attain heats much higher than the others can, no matter what they try."

"But how can they work in these temperatures?" She turned to look at him and was surprised that he didn't look nearly as hot as she did.

"Gnomes can tolerate a larger range of temperatures than we can. It's part of their physiology."

Saphira looked at the large pots and saw the ore melting in them. They seemed to be in various stages of preparation. Some had large chunks of ore just starting to melt. Others had workers surrounding it, carefully separating the gold from the other elements. The remaining pots held dissolving chunks of metal mixing in with the gold, forming several different shades of yellow.

Jack pointed to the last group and said, "Silver and copper work best with gold, but your hair had a few colors we couldn't replicate with those bases. They were subtle differences, but without them your hair would have looked flat, and that was unacceptable. They had particular trouble trying one mixture, and it turned explosive." Jack chuckled as he looked around the room. "It was a mess in here. Gold was over everything and everyone. It was a week before the air lost its golden hue."

"Were they okay?" Saphria asked.

"Who?" Jack looked back at Saphira.

"The gnomes."

Jacked waved his hand to the side. "Oh, they were fine. They only suffered a few burns and one or two lost some limbs because of it, but it was all worth it in the end. We were able to achieve a match that was closer than even I dared to hope. A true master sacrifices everything in their pursuit of perfection."

Saphira suddenly felt like throwing up. The room was beginning to blend itself together as the mental picture tilted to its side. "Could we finish this conversation somewhere else?" she asked faintly.

Jack looked at her, "Of course. You must be hot. I came here so often before your arrival that I got used to how warm it can get in here, but you haven't had time to adjust. We'll leave." He took her hand and led her back into the hallways.

It was so cold in comparison, she shivered involuntarily. Jack looked at her. "Are you okay?"

Her surroundings were already stabilizing themselves. "Yes. I think I just need to go back to my room and lay down for a while and recover."

Jack helped her walk back to her room and lifted the bed covers for her. After she lay down, Jack took her shoes off and then slid the blankets around her body. When he was satisfied that she was wrapped tight, he kissed her forehead. "Sleep tight," he said before shutting the door behind him. But sleep didn't come.

Did Jack really say the things she thought he did? She couldn't believe that the man she had agreed to marry and thought she knew so well could talk so nonchalantly about what the poor gnomes had suffered just to get another shade of yellow. Their pain had been completely unnecessary. She had never thought Jack could be so unfeeling towards someone else's pain – anyone's pain.

It took her a while to compose herself and rid herself of the heat-induced headache. It really had been so hot in there. How could anyone get used to it? Maybe she had misunderstood what he said. That's the only thing that would make sense. After all, one couldn't be so loving towards one person and yet so dismissive of another. Could they?

And he did love her. The statue, all the gifts he had given her, making sure she had the best of everything, they were all signs of his love. *So why does it feel wrong?* Saphira bit her lip.

If he had changed, then was it a result of being here, or his new position? Would her other friends have changed, too? Could the lack of sun be harmful to humans? She needed someone to talk to, but there was no one she could confide in. Elena was still out there, missing somewhere, and her parents couldn't help her anymore.

Saphira shook her head. She was an adult now. She could figure it out on her own. Tomorrow, she'd be able to think clearly, and she would know what her old friends thought about life here. They might be able to help her pinpoint the source of her growing uneasiness. Once she knew that, she could decide what to do next. She yawned and finally fell asleep.

Secret Passage

"Wow, that's amazing," Elena said as the dragon turned towards her. He had transformed again. He now came up to Elena's ear. His ears fanned out away from his face, and his long, muscular arms ended in clawed fingernails. The whites of his eyes were a pale yellow, and his skin was a light golden brown. "You look just like a gnome."

"It's not perfect, but it is easier to change back to your original form than any other shape." He grabbed a torch and handed it to Elena.

"Your original form? You used to be a gnome?"

"Of course," he said as he began to lead her through the various rooms of his cave. "All dragons used to be something. Most of the dragons are just so old they've forgotten what they used to be."

"When you became a dragon, did you change your name, too?"

"Why would I do that?"

"Because…you changed."

Damien shook his head. "Not where it counted." He opened a door and motioned for her to be quiet. "Remember what I said about doing what I do when you go through these next few rooms. If you don't, then I will not be held responsible for what happens to you." Elena nodded, and he went through the door, immediately turned to his right, and followed the wall to a hole on the other side.

The next room they passed on the left side, the room after that, they crossed on their backs. As they were making their way across the room, Elena asked, "Why did you decide to become a dragon?"

"It was the prudent thing to do."

Elena waited for a moment before asking, "Can anyone become a dragon?"

"In theory, yes. If an individual is willing to learn, then there is nothing to stop them from becoming a dragon. The first dragon had to discover it on his own, but it is a lot easier if you have someone to help you through the process."

"What is the process like?"

Damien sighed heavily. "Look at the ceiling." Several large cones came to a sharp point above their head. If Elena stood up, then she could easily touch them with her hands. "The process is like those stalactites. Your knowledge base must be large and complete before you can start. You learn everything's purposes – what they do, how they work, and how that can benefit you. Eventually, you will see connections, and your knowledge circle begins to condense. You see shorter routes and faster processes to create what you want. As your wisdom increases, you learn how to transform, fly, preserve life...everything.

"Many people become satisfied and stop there. They become your magicians and sorcerers. But there are a very few who continue to study until, eventually, their stalactite is a sharp point, and the difference between wanting and achieving is almost nonexistent."

"How long have you wanted to be a dragon?"

"I didn't want to. It had to. It was the only way."

"How long have you been a dragon, then?"

"For longer than I care to remember." They reached the end of the room and stood up. Before them was a barred door. "Do you have any other questions for me, or are you ready to go?"

"I'm ready." Elena breathed in deeply as she looked at this last door. "Let's go."

"Then this is your last reminder. Once I open this door, any sound we make will be increased. Do not speak at all unless I speak first, not even to call out in pain if you hurt something. This route will take us to the Trevastan dungeons. Do you understand?"

"Yes," Elena nodded.

"And you still want to go?"

"Absolutely."

Damien nodded and took her torch. He lit it with a small puff of flame from his mouth and handed it back to Elena who handled it cautiously. He then moved the big wooden planks that barred the door and opened it. Cold air blew into the chamber and Elena shivered in the thick cloak Damien had provided. They entered the darkness, and Elena slowly followed Damien as they worked their way down the passageway.

The roof was so low she bumped her head against the ceiling. She rubbed the top of her scalp. "Now I know why you made yourself so short."

"Quit talking and protect that light," Damien hissed. "I can't light it again in this passageway. Without it, you'll like this tunnel even less." Elena nodded and shielded the light from the breeze that threatened to consume her fire. Her mouth moved in a silent prayer that she would survive to see sunlight again.

Breaking Up Is Hard To Do

Lunch was held in a giant pleasure garden. To enter, they passed under a trellis where an ivy produced apple-like fruits. At the base, pale yellow blossoms were striped in pale orange. Their perfume, when she got close enough to smell it, made her forget everything else.

Saphira slowly spun around in a circle. Planters were spread throughout the room, and the base of each one was covered by a brightly colored fungus. Rising from those containers was the largest assortment of plants Saphira had ever seen.

"This is the most amazing garden I've ever seen," Saphira said as Jack came up to her carrying a tin cup.

"And most of it is edible, too. All it's missing is Elena's maze, and it would be perfect." Saphira blushed, and Jack laughed at her. "Come, let me help you pick out some plants to try."

"Oh no, I couldn't possibly eat anything as lovely as these."

"If you don't, then you will be missing a real treat." He picked leaves, berries, and nuts off the various plants and placed them in her cup.

"Did you know that gnomes have a whole underground agricultural department? These plants are their biggest success stories. This one," Jack said, pointing to a bush that produced small purple berries, "grows near our limestone hot springs, and this one," he pointed to the small-leafed plant next to it, "prefers the dry heat of our lava room."

"This little beauty here," he said, indicating a plant whose tips curved into delicate pink question marks and drooped with pale yellow, crescent shaped fruits, "loves fire ash." He picked off a moon and handed it to Saphira. "Its fruit is considered a delicacy. Would you like to try one?"

"Yes, please. Thank you," Saphira said as Jack handed it to her.

She tried it and spat it out immediately, but the taste didn't leave. It was sour and hot. Very, very hot. Tears began to roll down her face as Saphira waved cool air into her open mouth.

Jack laughed, and handed her a leaf. "Here, this will help."

She stuffed it in her mouth and began chewing. The heat began to subside, but only enough to stop the tears.

Jack led her to a small nook where tables and chairs had been set up. He grabbed a cup and pushed it through an opening in the wall. It filled up with some liquid and she swallowed it as soon as Jack handed it to her. Water spilled down the sides of her face, but she didn't care. All she cared about was quenching the fire in her mouth.

Jack smiled at her. "I think it's a little strong too, but the gnomes love it."

"You could have warned me," Saphira growled.

"I know, but I really wanted to see your face. I promise you, nothing else will take quite as much getting used to as the moonbow."

Saphira punched his arm, and Jack laughed. The door opened, and Saphira recognized two of the faces coming in. "Angela! Casper!" She ran up to them. She had never seen them wearing so many jewels before and both of them wore fine gloves to match their decadent clothes. Behind them stood two gnome servants. She wrapped Angela in a huge hug and was shocked at how skinny Angela had become. (She didn't think Angela could get any skinnier). Casper's quiet greeting made her worry if something was wrong with him, too. He assured her they were fine, but she watched them closely as they walked slowly to the seats. Their servants filled up their cups with plants to produce their own unique salads.

After them, ten other people joined them for lunch. Saphira almost cried every time someone new came in. She enjoyed her food much better than she thought she would and couldn't get her old friends to talk enough. Jack smiled as Saphira asked them question after question about what they did, how they liked it here, what their impressions were of the gnomes…everything. She also asked about the attack and who hadn't made it.

When they confirmed her parents had died, she nodded sadly. She knew, but there was a small part of her that had hoped Jack's information was wrong. She was able to hold the tears in until they mentioned the other victims. She had known all of them. They hadn't needed to die either. Angela came over and kept an arm around Saphira until the tear flow became controlled and gentle.

Concerning life here, all the answers were positive and consisted of the same themes: their initial impression of the gnomes was horribly wrong and nothing could be better than the life they had here among the gnomes.

The longer they spoke, the more Saphira began to suspect there was something they weren't telling her. When she asked about Elena's family, they looked at each other before Casper informed her that they wanted to be here but were currently caught up in some "pressing business." She was told other survivors she missed had chosen to "go home." She asked for more details, but they took one look at Jack and refused to elaborate.

"Jack," she asked after the townspeople had left, "did you notice anything different about them?"

"What do you mean?"

Saphira struggled for the words to properly express her feelings, but failed. "I don't know. They just seem changed somehow. People who were very open and friendly now seem more… guarded."

"People change. It happens. Remember, you haven't seen them for months. You can't expect them to be exactly the same as you left them."

"But why weren't they happy to see you again? They barely talked to you."

"That's not true. Remember, they've talked to me on several occasions. It's *you* they haven't seen in a while. Of course they are going to pay more attention to you initially. It's the way things go."

"But they've also lost so much weight. Is something the matter with them?"

"Nonsense. That's just your imagination. Some people might have lost a *little* weight, but we eat a lot more fruits and vegetables down here than they were used to. Some weight loss is to be expected."

Saphira shook her head. "There is more to it than that," she whispered to herself. She didn't trust his answers. He refused to consider that something might not be right. Saphira wondered what their lives were really like. Life here was not good for them, no matter what they, or Jack, said.

As for Jack, she had to finally admit that there was something different about the Jack she knew and the Jack that stood before her. He *had* changed, and she didn't know if she could live with those changes.

"Jack," she said after a pause, "I can't stay here any longer. I have to go."

"Of course, my dear," Jack said as he stood up, "I will take you back to your room."

"No. I want to go back home – out of the mountains."

"Why? What could you possibly want there that we don't have here?"

"Light, air, I don't know," Saphira said. "I can't tell you why I want to leave so much, because I don't fully know myself. It's a lot of little things, and it's more a series of impressions than any solid complaints. All the gnomes I have met have been more than courteous, and everyone who was at that lunch had wonderful things to say, but it just doesn't feel right to me somehow."

Jack didn't seem perturbed by her reaction at all. "I had hoped you could grow to love it here as much as I, but I won't force us to live here, if you don't like it. I will talk to King Brackster tomorrow about becoming an ambassador to King Cedric. I'm sure there would be room for us in the castle. It's an impressive building. Have I ever told you about it?"

Saphira shook her head. She didn't want to tell him that she had already seen it and become intimately acquainted with its dungeon section.

"I didn't get a chance to see too much of it the last time I was there, but it has all the air and light you could ask for. We will leave the day after our wedding if you still want to go."

"That's another thing I wanted to talk with you about." Saphira studied her hands. "I don't think there is going to be a wedding anymore."

Jack put his hand under her head and lifted her chin. His eyes studied hers intensely. "What do you mean?"

"The more I see of you, the more I realize I no longer have a place with you anymore."

"That's ridiculous. Don't you know how much I idolize and adore you? Love is forever."

"Do you even know who I am anymore?" Saphira asked. "I feel like a prized puppy. I want to be someone's *companion*, not their pet. There are moments when I feel that level of connection we used to share, but they are becoming less and less frequent. And worst of all, I don't feel like I know you anymore.

"It's difficult to describe, but I feel like there is a barrier between us that wasn't there before. I hear you, and I see you, but I don't feel like I know what you're thinking. You've changed, and I can't explain how, but I don't know this new part of you. When I agreed to marry you, I thought I knew your soul, that I was familiar with all the different parts of your personality. Not anymore. There is a part of you that I don't understand and that doesn't coincide with what I remember of you. I will always love you, but I can't commit myself to the stranger you've become."

"I see." Jack took both her hands gently in his. "I was going to wait to tell you this, but I won't. I think it will explain some of the things you've been sensing about me. There *is* something different about me that I've been hiding from you.

"I have been changed. No, it's more than that. I've been transformed. It has been wonderful, and it's a blessing I can give to you as well. I used to be subject to thousands of limitations on my body and soul, hampering my potential, but because of the graciousness of my king, I have been given the means to rise above them all. Once you experience it for yourself you will know what I am talking about. You will become something more than human, and we will be equals again."

Saphira was scared as she looked into his eyes that were intense and frenzied at the same time. "What, exactly, happened to you?"

"It was something wonderful. I can't describe it all, but it took place shortly after I saved Brackster from the assassination plot. It was part of my reward. I was taken to a special room. He said a few sacred words over me, and I suddenly felt alive, better than I have ever felt before. Not only was my body invigorated, but my mind as well. I knew things I hadn't known before, and I was filled with wisdom. In just a few seconds I went from being an average human, to something more. Something better. I don't know all the changes that occurred, but I no longer have to fear death and separation from you ever again if you accept these blessings as well."

Saphira was horrified. "You can't die?" She tried to take her hands back, but he tightened his grip just enough to stop her.

"No. Isn't that wonderful? You and I could live together in perfect love. Just imagine, you can become my real Rhonda, and we could reign together forever. Death which destroys all other loves could never touch ours. No mortal cares or concerns could distract us from what is most important. We can remain as perfect as we are right now."

"Is the king 'perfected' as well?"

"Gnomes can't hold the transformation. They get sick. He has been looking a long time to find someone worthy to hold the gift. When we met, he knew he had found his perfect candidate: someone who would keep and hold the kingdom the way it should be held. A man who could bring this kingdom back to its days of glory."

"What are you talking about?"

"Saphira, do you realize what we humans have done? There was a time when gnomes and humans used to live in peace. When humans first arrived in these lands, gnomes welcomed us, gave us homes, and taught us how to survive. How do you think they were able to make such perfect reproductions of the animals or the fields at harvest time? It's because they used to live there. That menagerie room is more than just a work of art, it is a sign of their heritage and where they will be again."

"Be again? When? The people will never give it up."

"They will have to. It belongs to the gnomes. It's a matter of justice. You've seen the animals. You've seen the tapestries. You know I speak the truth, and King Cedric will too. He cannot deny it. If he tries, then a little force might be required, but our claim will not be denied."

"A little force?" Saphira yelled as she ripped her hands away from him. "It would be war. King Cedric would never agree to hand everything over. It's been too long. Nobody knows anything about the things you claim as facts."

"But it *is* the truth! That knowledge came as part of the enlightenment I received when I was changed. When the war is over, everything will be the way it is supposed to be. Gnomes will live and work under the sky as they were intended to. But don't worry. We will be kinder to the humans than they were to us. Humans will be allowed to live instead of chased to near extinction. If they accept the new rule, then they may even rise in the ranks of the new government, just like I did. True equality and peace could be had at last."

"If you do establish peace, then it would be the peace of a dictator, and that is not something I can support. Your transformation has killed your sense of decency and compassion. I would rather die than become what you have become."

Jack pressed against Saphira as she tried to back away. Her eyes widened as she looked up into Jack's eyes, filled with hate towards her for the first time. His pupils grew larger and larger until all the color that had been in his eyes disappeared. Where his pupils had been there was a hint of flames and blue fire. "You are wrong. You will beg for my forgiveness when the truth is forced upon you," he hissed.

"Guards!" Jack's voice reverberated off the walls, and a contingent of guards came running up to them quickly. "Escort Saphira back to her chambers. I have some preparations to make for a pre-wedding ceremony, and I want her to be kept safe until it is ready and I come for her." He handed her over to the care of the guards who escorted her back to her room.

She flung herself on her bed and let the tears flow around her unanswered question: "Where did it all go wrong?" She had lost her parents, lost Jack, and was about to be turned into something horrible.

Transformation

The next morning her eyes felt heavy and stiff. She groaned as she realized she was still alive. She wished she had died with her illusion of Jack. After she splashed water on her face, she looked at herself in the mirror. The night spent crying had taken its toll. Her eyes were red, hidden under thick, puffy lids. She looked awful and felt the same way. What had just happened? What was going to happen? Was she awaiting a fate worse than death? How could she escape? She didn't want to know anything more about Jack's "glorious transformation." Nothing good could have produced such a negative effect on Jack's behavior and personality. If she had any more tears to shed, then she might have cried again, but she didn't.

The only way out of the room was through the door that had been locked since they brought her back. She was pretty sure there was a guard posted outside her door as well. Even if she managed to slip past him, then she had no chance of getting out of the mountain undetected. If she tried and failed, then she had no idea how this new Jack would punish her.

Although, how could it possibly be worse than what he was going to do now? She lay back down on her bed. She stared at the ceiling and tried to think of her options. Had she missed something? What could she do to avoid being changed?

Saphira heard the sounds of someone shifting positions in the hallway. She sat up and looked with interest at the door. There was a knock, and Jack walked into the room. He walked over to Saphira, still dressed in the clothes she had worn the day before, and sat down beside her. He tried to take her hand, but she crossed her arms and turned her back to him.

"Don't be angry with me, Saphira. I'm sorry I lost my temper. I forgot that these realizations can take time to sink in. It can be hard to accept the fact that humans have not been perfect."

"That's not what I have issues with. I know we are not perfect but neither are the gnomes. There are issues that need to be resolved, it's true, but there are other ways to solve the grievances." She turned her shoulder just enough to see him again. "The Jack I know would have found those."

"But I am your Jack. Look at me." He touched his hands to his chest. "I'm the same person."

Saphira turned completely around. "No, you're not. Physically, you're the same, and sometimes you act like the Jack I knew and loved, but there are times when you turn into another person entirely. Your lack of patience and mercy is appalling. You have become a miserable being."

To her surprise, Jack didn't get mad. He just touched her shoulder and smiled. "That's what you say now, but I trust that by this evening you will be friendlier towards me. For now, you have an engagement this afternoon that I won't let you miss." His hand squeezed her shoulder gently. "I suggest you put on a new outfit for it."

"Hmmph." Saphira shrugged him off.

Jack laughed before heading to the door. He rapped lightly on its frame, and the door opened for him. "I'll see you soon, my beauty." Jack winked at her before exiting.

Determined not to do anything he would like, Saphira crossed her legs and sat in the middle of the bed. She heard a second knock, and Rapella slowly entered the room.

"What are you doing here?" Saphira asked.

Rapella curtseyed deeply and said apologetically, "I am here to help you get ready. I was told to make sure you looked your best for today's activities."

The sympathy in her voice led Saphira to hope. She scooted to the edge of her bed and pled in a whispered voice, "Please, you have to help me. There's something wrong with Jack. He's not acting right, and I don't trust whatever he has planned for me. I'm not safe here. You have to help me escape."

Rapella shook her head sadly. "I'm sorry miss, but my orders are to not to do anything of the kind."

"Then I'm giving you new orders."

Rapella looked at the floor. "I'm sorry miss, but I dare not do that."

"Then 'dare' something!" Saphira punched the bed on her way up and began to pace the room. "You could say I'm too sick to go, or that all my dresses are ruined, or that I twisted my ankle… anything to delay what's coming next."

"I'm sorry Ma'am. It won't work."

"You are good for nothing. Do you know that?" Saphira walked past Rapella to the other side of the room.

Rapella sighed and picked the bathrobe and the dark blue dress out of the closet and brought it over to Saphira. "Please, Ma'am, I have orders. I can't go against them. I wish I could, but if I don't get you ready, then…"

Saphira looked back over her shoulder and sighed. Rapella's face was clearly pleading, her eyes wide and dewy with contained tears. "Fine," she finally agreed.

She offered no resistance as Rapella changed her dress for a new one, but no aid either. Rapella then wrapped the bathrobe around Saphira and washed her hair. It did not feel as luxurious as it had the last time she had done it. When she was done, Rapella combed it out and began to style it as Saphira said, "I'm sorry, I know I shouldn't take out my frustration on you. It's not your fault, but can't you do anything?"

"I wish I could. I hate to see you so upset," Rapella said as she twisted Saphira's hair on top of her head.

"Is there no hope for me then?"

"Of course there's hope. Maybe you were wrong? Lord Kinyard is powerful, good looking, and dedicated to you. Surely, it can't be as bad as you are fearing."

"I wish I could convince myself that my intuition is wrong and things are going to be well, but it's impossible."

Saphira didn't say any more until Rapella finished. Had it been any other day, or any other situation, Saphira would have liked the effect Rapella created with her hair.

"I suppose I should say thank you," Saphira said. "But right now, I would just like some time alone."

"Of course, my lady." Rapella withdrew, and Saphira was left alone again. She got up and began to pace. "I wish I knew what to do." When she put her hands in the robe pockets, she felt the diviner. Smiling, she pulled it out. "I need another perspective. Oh diviner, what do I do now?"

She was interrupted by a knock on the door. Saphira panicked and shoved the diviner down the front of her dress as Jack strolled into the room. When he entered, he paused, looked around and sniffed. He walked slowly around the room, occasionally glancing at Saphira.

When he had finished his circuit, he looked at her and said, "Hand over the robe." Saphira handed it to him, and he checked the pockets. She was glad she hadn't put the diviner back where she had gotten it. When he was done, he apologized, "Sorry. I just thought I sensed…something." He looked around one last time, before giving up and focused in on Saphira again.

"You look stunning. I'm glad you let Rapella help you get ready." He touched her neck, and Saphira moved her head away from him. Jack laughed. "You tease. Come, we don't want to be late." He held out his arm, but Saphira ignored him. Holding her head high she walked to the door. He opened it for her, and she swept past him into the hall. She lifted her skirts slightly in case the hallway was clear, and she could run, but guards waited for her – five on either side of the door. When she paused, Jack joined her and offered her his arm.

"I'm afraid we are going somewhere you haven't been to yet so you will have to let me escort you there." She ignored his arm, and he continued, "You can take my arm and walk with me, or a guard will pick you up and carry you there. I think you would prefer to walk. They would not be gentle." Saphira glared at him before taking his arm.

After they had gone a couple of yards, the guards began to follow them. She glanced back several times, but the guards maintained the same distance behind them.

"I know what you're thinking." Jack whispered to her. She jumped and looked at him. "You are wondering why they are so far away from us. Their distance is practiced and intentional. They are too far away to understand what we say if we whisper, but the slowest of them could overtake you in five seconds if you started to run."

Saphira looked back again and remembered how fast they had traveled down the tunnels when they brought her in. Returning her gaze to Jack, she said, "I hate you."

Jack laughed, "I know you do." He then continued in a more somber tone, "This may all seem a little hard right now, but that is because you fear what you do not understand. If the benefits wouldn't be so great, I wouldn't force you to do it. It's like when your mother forces you to take your medicine. The medicine I'm offering will cure all your pains forever. You are an amazing woman, and you deserve all the benefits this can bring you. I can't just let you go."

They walked away from the artist's studios and deeper into the depths of the castle. Eventually they stopped in front of one of the plainly decorated doors that lined the hallway.

She heard some rattling noises, but couldn't place the sound before Jack opened the door and led Saphira in. There was a chair in the corner, and Jack held it out for her. She sat down with as much dignity as she could manage and looked around.

The room had just one entrance. The walls were clean and smooth, but there was a small puddle of water in the corner of the room. When the door closed, the room would become very, very dark.

"Where are we?"

"The transformation room."

"This is the room? I was expecting something grander. This is more like a cell than anything else."

"Yes, well, the room was moved here after the first couple of transformations didn't go as planned."

"What do you mean?" Saphira looked around the cell and noticed small claw marks on the walls. Her eyes widened.

"I did tell you gnomes don't always come through the transformation successfully, didn't I? Failed merges are not pretty and never safe for the bystanders."

"So you would just leave them here until they died if something went wrong?" Saphira tried to stand, but Jack pressed her back down against the seat.

"Don't worry. I would never allow this to happen if there was the least chance something might not go right with the process."

Saphira twisted her head until she was looking in his eyes again. "What if this whole transformation process is wrong?"

Jack shook his head, but otherwise ignored her question. "It might take awhile for you to become adjusted to the change, but I will see you when this is all over."

He tried to kiss her lips, but she turned her head. Laughing quietly at her, he kissed her cheek. Then he left, shutting the door behind him. Saphira stood up and silently moved towards the door. She felt along the edges and pushed on the slats, but it was now a solid part of the wall. She began kicking and punching the door, pressing against it with all her might, but there was not the slightest give anywhere in its sturdy frame. She paused to get her breath.

In the quiet, she thought she detected chanting coming from the other side. She would have to find another way out. She moved over to the nearby wall. The moisture had to collect from somewhere. She searched for small holes, loose rocks, and anything else that indicated erosion.

As she passed by the puddle, she was distracted by a faint ripple that spread across its face. It was a barely visible black on black movement. As the chanting continued, the puddle grew. Not just out, but up. She barely noticed when the voice stopped because there, standing in front of her, was something that resisted all illumination. Near the top of the form, a pair of crimson red eyes popped open and stared at Saphira. It smiled, revealing a set of white pointed teeth. Those became the only two colors in the room. Saphira screamed.

She ran over to the door and pounded with renewed fury. "Out! Let me out of here, NOW!"

Her words jumbled into a single, terrified syllable that caused Jack, who had reached the end of the hallway, to pause. He smiled as if the sound were music to his ears and continued on his way.

Navestrung

Elena and Damien were nearing the end of the tunnel when they heard the scream. "Did you hear that? It's Saphira, we've got to get her." The last few hours in the tunnel had been awful. It had gotten narrower and lower. Even Damien was stooping now.

"No. It's too late," Damien said, grabbing hold of Elena. "There's nothing we can do for her."

"They're torturing her. We have to stop it!" Elena said, trying to get out of his grip.

"No, they aren't."

"Then why would she scream?"

"That was a scream of terror, not pain. The only thing that would produce that level of fear in her is a demon."

"We have to stop it."

"We can't. It is the one thing in these mountains that should be feared more than me."

"But you're a dragon. Can't you just eat it or something?"

"What is it with you and having me eat things? We have other offensive weapons you know. But even if I was face to face with one and wanted to eat it, I couldn't. Demons aren't like anything you've ever seen before. Traditional means of attack do nothing to them. By themselves, they have no real substance. They are not harmed by things that hurt the rest of us. Saphira's only hope would have been the shakra. But they would not have handed her over to the demon if she still had it with her."

"What will it do to her?"

"It will enter her body. There it will compete with her soul for control. If it wins, then she will become a navestrung."

Elena gasped and stared towards where the sound had come from. "Oh, my poor Saphira."

"She will look like herself, she will talk like herself, she will even have the same memories, but it will all be under the control of the demon."

Elena's eyebrows knit together. "She would still look like herself? I always pictured them as huge, grotesque monsters. I never realized they could be humans."

Damien shook his head. "Once they bond, they are no longer human."

"How would the shakra stop it?"

"I don't know exactly how it works, I just know that it does. It prevents the demon from entering or physically harming that person's body, even if they've been invited."

"Saphira would never ask a demon to come into her body!"

Damien shrugged his shoulders. "Then someone invoked one on her behalf. The spell that calls them prepares the host's mind and empowers the demon to bind with a body."

"What would happen if she had the shakra?"

"It would attack her mentally. It would manipulate what she saw and heard, hoping she would fling the shakra away in confusion. If that didn't work, it would look for a new body it could enter. However, that new being wouldn't be prepared to house it, and the host's mind would be shredded."

Elena shivered. "Thanks for the warning." She thought for a moment before asking, "Where do they usually hold these transformations?"

"The dungeons. This way if the transformation doesn't hold, then they don't have to move the deranged thing the demon leaves behind."

"So, the room would probably have a thick door, right?"

"Yes....What are you getting at?"

"We could at least go and see what has become of her, can't we? I'm sure they have some kind of protections set up so the demon won't be able to get us from the other side of the door. If it alerts the others to my presence, then it doesn't matter. I was going to reveal myself sooner or later."

"I wouldn't recommend doing that. You would think she's fine in there, but she won't be. She will betray you or attack you outright once she's free if she thinks she has the advantage. You should just accept the fact that your friend is lost and move on."

"No. I came all the way here. I am not turning back until I know she is really gone."

"Fine," Damien said. "I'll take you inside their dungeons. I'll even confirm her status for you, but you will have to believe me. If I say she is gone, then you have to leave her. She will use whatever tactic she can to get out of the room. Do not disobey me, or you will die. I know what's on the other side of the door better than you do."

"Thank you, Damien." Elena went to give him a hug, but Damien stopped her.

"Don't thank me yet."

They traveled a dozen more yards before Damien motioned that they had gone far enough. Damien had Elena cover the lamp with the cloak and place it on the ground. Damien stood at the end of the tunnel and pushed in a stalactite. Elena heard a slight creak, and an impression of light created a line down the front of the tunnel's wall. Damien tilted his head to a side, listening, before pushing on the wall where the light appeared.

The crack widened, and Elena saw that it marked the edges of a big stone door. On the other side of the door was a long hallway. There were several doors along each side of the hallway. The doors all had small windows with bars across the top and handles protruding from small moveable sections of wood a quarter of the way off the floor.

Damien held his finger to his mouth as they glided down the hall, barely making a sound. As they passed each door, Elena could hear mutterings, moans, and the occasional clink of metal against rock coming from inside the rooms.

At the end of the hallway, they saw a series of plain wooden doors. Damien whispered, "This is where they used to call the demons. You go first and tell me if you hear your friend." They passed in front of the doors one by one. Most of them were quiet, but behind one of them was the sound of heavy breathing.

"Do you think she could be in here?" Elena whispered to Damien.

"Elena?" Saphira asked.

"Yes," Elena replied cautiously.

"Get out of here now."

Elena pressed herself against the door. "What's going on?"

"Something evil. I can't explain beyond that."

"Are you okay in there?"

"No, there's something else in here. It doesn't like me, but it *really* doesn't like you. I don't know exactly what it's doing, but I can sense its growing agitation."

"This can't be," Damien said quickly, coming in closer. "She still has the shakra. The demon hasn't entered her body yet."

"Who's that?"

"A friend," Elena replied.

"How did you get in here with the shakra?" Damien demanded.

"You mean my diviner? They didn't know I had it."

"They didn't sense it?"

"Jack might have. He was acting really weird. He made me hand over the robe I was wearing and emptied its pockets.

He probably would have done the same to my dress, except it doesn't have any pockets."

"Jack?" Elena asked.

"Yes. You are not going to believe this, but Jack's alive. He's somewhere in the city, but they've done something to him. He's evil. If you see him, then you have to run."

"Do you want to get out of there, Saphira?" Damien asked.

"Yes."

"Then listen to me carefully. We don't have much time before they come back and check on you. There are some things I need you to understand. First, your 'diviner' is a shakra, and second, the thing in there with you is a demon. It has no body, but it is filled with profound hatred. If it gets the chance, then it will kill you. It cannot while you have the shakra, but if we open this door before it has been defeated, Elena will be destroyed. Do you understand?"

"Yes," Saphira replied shakily.

"Good. Then take the shakra and hold it in your hand. Put your other hand over the top and hold it up to your eye so you can still see the shakra, but nothing else. Have you done that?"

"Yes."

"I need you to concentrate on the shakra. Do you remember when you activated it at the campfire? Can you see the way the fire lit up the stone in your mind? Those extra bits of light still reside inside. You just need to draw it out. Imagine scooping inside and pulling it towards the surface. Keep doing that until it begins to spill over into your hands."

Saphira did as she was told and was astonished as the area between her palms grew lighter. There was no way this could be a reflection. The shakra was creating its own light. It was like holding a miniature sun ball.

The demon shifted away from Saphira. It began hissing and screeching. Saphira looked up and scanned her cell, trying to pinpoint the demon.

"Saphira, ignore him and focus on that light. Remember what it looks like and feels like," Damien reprimanded.

Saphira looked back at her shakra and noticed that its glow had faded in the short time she had looked away from it. She focused again on drawing out its energy. The demon continued to manipulate the environment, but the shakra grew steadily brighter.

"You're doing great, Saphira. This next part is extremely tricky, and you can't let anything the demon might do take your mind from the task before you. Remember, he cannot physically harm you. What I need you to do now is to look at the shakra. You need to move beyond light's physical properties. Think about what produces inner radiance. Do you think you can do that? Try to pull *that* out now."

"I'll try." Saphira looked at the shakra and thought of all the goodness she had known and the personalities of those who radiated light and joy.

The room was suddenly filled with creatures of all shapes and sizes. There were bats with high pitched squeals circling the roof of the room before swooping down, narrowly missing Saphira's head, the breeze from their descent ruffling her hair. Hungry eyes and pale teeth gleamed at her from the corners of the room. She could also feel icy cold tendrils of breath reaching down the nape of her dress.

Shivering, she brought her hands closer to her face so all she could see was what was inside her hands. Everything except Damien's voice began to fade into the background.

"Good, now imagine all that warmth settling on the demon."

Saphira did as she was told, and she was so focused on maintaining the glow that she barely registered when the other noises faded into an agonized rasp. It wasn't until Elena was alternating between shaking and hugging her that she looked up from her palms.

"Saphira! I'm so happy to see you again, are you all right?"

Saphira looked around the room and realized the demon was gone.

"Yes, I guess I am."

"Come, we must go." Damien extended his hand towards Saphira as he glanced around the room. "It's not safe here and there is much you need to learn."

Saphira just looked at Damien. "Why are you helping us? How did you meet Elena?"

"Listen, I will answer your questions, but not now and not here. All you need to know is that I mean you no harm." Saphira still didn't move, so he grabbed her hand and dragged her after him back to the tunnel. Elena followed.

Damien closed the tunnel door behind them. "We'll wait in here until the guards have come and gone. Saphira, I think you had better tell us what happened to you after you became separated from Elena."

They listened in silence as Saphira whispered her tale to them in the darkness of the tunnel. When she got to the part about Jack's personality changes, his sudden temper, and how his eyes changed, Damien asked what had set him off, but otherwise remained silent.

"That's everything. What happened to you after we were separated?" Saphira asked Elena.

"I followed your trail until it came to the mine entrance and realized that I wouldn't be able to follow you in there. I went back to the camp, found some jewels the gnomes had missed, and headed to the Northern Cave. That's where I met Damien. He's a dragon, and he led me here along the tunnels."

"He's a dragon?" Saphira peeked at Damien. "I thought they were supposed to look different. He doesn't look like he can fly. Are all gnomes dragons?"

"No, dragons are shape-shifters. This just happens to be what he looks like now. When I first met him he looked like a human. At least he did from a distance. I guess that's why people thought they were extinct. They were looking for a big flying beast, not another gnome or human, or whatever else they can become."

"Appearances can be very deceiving," Damien agreed.

"I'm just glad you didn't get captured," Saphira said. "After I found out the truth about Jack, I felt sick about sending you a letter inviting you to come down. Did you see it, or had you already set out to rescue me at that point."

Elena shook her head. "We had already left, but I probably wouldn't have seen it anyway. The entrance to the cave is so dark you can't see anything on the other side. At least I couldn't. When I went inside, I felt like I was walking into pitch-black evilness." Elena shivered.

"It's one of the defenses I put on my home," Damien explained. "Gnomes have developed a healthy fear of dragons and anything they associate with us."

"Yes, I know. Jack yelled at them when they even mentioned the word dragon. He said they were crazy for thinking dragons were still around."

"But it turns out they were right. Damien showed me this back way into their city and helped me rescue you. I wouldn't have known what to do without him," Elena said.

"Yes, thank you," Saphira said to Damien.

"Nonsense. We just opened the door; you saved yourself," Damien responded curtly.

"So, what do we do now?" Saphira asked.

"You need to learn how to master the shakra and quickly, but we don't have time to go back to my cave. We need to find a safe place here." Damien tapped his upper lip with his finger.

"What do you mean?"

Damien put his finger down and leaned towards her. "I mean, King Brackster is preparing for war. Navestrungs are too controversial. He wouldn't call them unless everything else was prepared. If you want any chance to stop him, then we must act now."

"There are navestrungs here?" Saphira glanced around terrified.

"Yes, Jack is one. His eyes gave him away."

"Impossible. He couldn't have been that evil." Saphira then remembered how he treated the gnomes and the veiled warnings from her friends. He had hidden it, but that must have been what his transformation was really about. She started to shiver uncontrollably and Elena wrapped her arms around her.

"What should we do?" Elena asked.

"We need to find a place where some teachings from the starlings still exist, where there are some protective shields against navestrungs, and where we won't be constantly in danger of being spied." Damien snapped his fingers. "That's it. We'll go to the heart. With any luck, Brackster won't even know of its existence, and we will have all the time we need there."

"The heart?"

"Yes. It's where the gnome resistance met during the Great War and where the starlings gave them their shakras."

Saphira's voiced squeaked, "What?"

"Not all gnomes sided with the navestrungs. They fought just as hard as Elexa to destroy the monsters. The protection spells enacted then should still be in place, and it is there that you can best learn to master its powers. If you want to get Jack back, then you will need all the help you can get."

"Then you think he can be saved?" Elena asked, placing a hand on Saphira's shoulder.

Damien nodded. "As long as he didn't invite the demon on his own, there are ways to separate them."

"How do we get there?" Saphira asked standing up.

Damien waved her down. "Give me a minute, and I will tell you. The memory lies a long way back, and I want to make sure I remember everything about that place: where it is, how to enter, and any possible traps." Damien, leaned against the wall and closed his eyes. Elena and Saphira looked at each other but remained silent.

A few minutes later, Damien opened his eyes and said, "I'm afraid I am only aware of one remaining entrance. We are not likely to go unnoticed."

"Then you go. You could pass through the streets undetected, and you know a lot more about the shakra than I do. Please, take it, stop the king, and set Jack free." Saphira tried to hand Damien the Shakra, but he rejected it.

"I'm sorry, but I cannot. Not all shakras are the same, and yours was designed to work with a human. I may take the form of a human, but I am not one. Ousting a demon that has settled in is extremely difficult. You will need to be there, not only because the stone belongs to you and your race, but also because you knew Jack before he became a navestrung. That will be essential knowledge if you want to save him."

Saphira's hand tightened around the shakra. "Then we'll go."

Elena turned to Damien, "Do you know any spells that could help?"

Damien shook his head. "I'm afraid to. Navestrungs would sense them right away. There are only certain areas down here where magic can be used freely."

There was silence for several moments before Elena asked, "Damien, how are humans usually treated? The mines are awful, but Saphira was treated well and she said the others didn't complain about their stay."

Damien snorted. "They probably didn't dare to. Humans are not treated well anywhere in our borders. With the exception of Saphira, once they're captured, they either slave in the mines, or slave in the noble's homes."

Saphira buried her head in her hands. She had known something wasn't right. "And what happens when they get in trouble?"

"It varies. The most common punishments include being whipped, branded, or locked in chains." He reached out and patted Saphira's shoulder awkwardly. "I'm sorry, but it's true."

"Don't be," Elena smiled, "I just thought of a way to get us in."

Saphira's head shot up. "How?" she and Damien asked together.

"Like this." She turned and sternly reprimanded her friend, "Saphira, how dare you try on your mistress's dress. Do you think you are as good as one of us? You have defiled it, and it is now only fit for the dogs." Elena picked up the edge of Saphira's dress before throwing it back down in fake disgust. "Since that is what you are, you can wear it if you wish. But you will be chained until the dress falls apart so that you will learn to associate pain with my clothes, and you will never be tempted to wear what does not belong to you ever again." Elena resumed her normal tone. "Do you think they'll buy it?"

Damien slowly smiled as he contemplated the plan. "Yes, I think it just might work. That would explain why Saphira would be wearing such a fine dress. What's your story Elena?"

"I got this one," Saphira said and began shaking her finger, "Elena, you ungrateful little wench. I feed you, I clothe you, and this is how you repay me? By running away? I will make sure you can't get away from me so fast in the future. I hope you enjoy your new leg wear."

"I like it, and I am escorting you back to your owners from the blacksmith's shop. There should be plenty of chains we can use in the dungeon."

"Perfect." Saphira clapped her hands together. "When can we leave?"

"After they've checked your cell. The guards who brought you here would recognize you in an instant. It's best to wait until they've gone to alert Jack of your absence. I will go out and get the chains while you two stay here. Elena, you won't have to do too much to your appearance because of the type of journey we had getting here, but Saphira, you need to rub that dirt in well. You are much, much too clean for a human. I'll help you make any last minute adjustments when I get back."

Heart Of The Mountain

Damien returned with two sets of ankle chains and some rope and examined the girls. Dirt tracks ran down their faces, and Saphira's hair was back to the shade she came into the mountains with. Damien helped them into the chains and linked them together with rope cuffs. He held on to the remaining length of rope.

"Now, we wait."

A few minutes later they heard a clamor of voices. The girls couldn't understand what they were saying so Damien whispered the gist of their conversation to them. "They were checking the progress of your transformation. You've just been discovered missing. Apparently Jack is going to be very angry with them when he finds out you're gone. They assume the demon did its job, and you escaped using some navestrung magic. Someone is going to run to inform Jack, and the others will look for clues to find out where you went."

When everything was quiet again, Damien said, "All right, I think it's safe for us to go. I don't think I need to remind you ladies to act beaten and subdued." They hung their heads low and shuffled their feet while Damien pulled on the rope that ran through their chains, connecting them together.

They didn't meet anyone in the first two halls they traveled down, but after that, they began meeting gnomes with much more frequency. Some of them stopped and asked what the offenses were. They clucked their tongues when they heard what the humans had done and praised the punishment.

"Good for their masters," one of them said. "I'll never understand why our king saw fit to raise one up so high. I cannot approve of it. Humans are lying, thieving, ungrateful scum — the whole pack of them." Elena's fist clenched together and Saphira bit her lip to keep herself from responding. She knew it wouldn't help their cause.

They traveled to the edge of the castle walls and followed its border towards the older section of the city. Smaller houses began merging with the wall, and Damien led them through the side door of one of them. Once inside, they couldn't be seen from the street and Damien removed their bindings. "I don't think we'll need these anymore."

He lifted a section of the floorboard to reveal a cellar. He helped them down to the ground before jumping. He landed with a soft thud. After replacing the floorboards, Damien walked to the wall and puffed his cheeks out. They began to glow and illuminated a section of the wall.

There were dozens of picture boards carved into the wall. Damien pressed against the second, third and fifth paintings before stepping back. A large rock slid into the wall, and then moved aside revealing a tunnel. Damien led the way inside, and the girls followed. It was more spacious than they were expecting.

"If you don't mind, then I would like to change back into my dragon form. It will help me be more aware of what is happening outside the tunnel, and I prefer it."

"I guess so," Saphira said.

"Then stay here. I'll travel forward until it will be safe for me to transform." He left them in the darkness, but Saphira felt the tunnel expand to accommodate Damien's new size. They followed the tunnel forward until they caught up to him, and Saphira almost choked when she saw him.

"You weren't kidding about the shape-shifting thing were you? You really are a dragon."

"Yes. I told you that."

"I just never quite believed it. You certainly look like a dragon now, however."

Damien sighed.

When they reached the heart, Saphira stopped staring at Damien. The room was not what she expected. It was completely round, and an ornate design radiated out from its center. Nothing else was in the room. They walked further inside and a rock slid in front of the tunnel they had just used. Except for a faint outline, it was impossible to distinguish from the surrounding walls. Damien blew out a faint purple fog that settled into the borders of the door before disappearing.

"What did you do?" Saphira asked.

"I created a temporary block on this door. It won't automatically open anymore."

"Could the gnomes follow us in here?" Elena eyed the walls suspiciously.

"Yes, but they would use the same entrance we did. I've bought us some time, but we need to get started right away. Saphira, take your shakra and move to the center circle on the floor. I need you to stand in the very middle of the design. Elena, go join her. That mark will help protect you when the time comes."

"Protect us from what?" Elena asked as she moved to the circle.

"From the very thing Saphira fought earlier. Hundreds of years ago, before the Great War began, tension between the races was strong. Each thought their kind was the best and refused to accept the good in others. Demons came into existence and fed off the bickering. Their leaders tried to establish peace and almost succeeded, but one misguided gnome was not content to live side-by-side with the others. He sought out the demons and agreed to let one of them enter his body in exchange for immortality and the power to make his vision come true.

"He came back and overthrew the king. He forced his top commanders to do as he had done and they called themselves, 'navestrungs.' He then armed his soldiers and set out with the sole desire to enslave all the other races to his will. The force of the navestrung strengthened army overwhelmed the other groups.

"Some gnomes defected and fought to stop the unnatural forces at work. It was then that the starlings gifted the world with the shakras. At first we thought they were just there to help guide us in our war. They helped us communicate with each other and gave us tips on where to hide and what tactics would win the next battle. But when a shakra-wielder was captured, we discovered that the starlings infused the shakras with more power than just their ability to predict the future. The shakras protected the wearer from possession. They could also kill navetrungs and drive the demons out of possessed bodies, but only if the host had resisted.

"There was finally an effective weapon against the navestrungs. As the beings were freed, they joined in the fight against the navestrungs and their army. Those who could master the shakras became our greatest warriors and best hope."

Saphira looked at her shakra in wonder as Damien continued, "As the tide turned in the battle, the gnome king experimented with binding other races. Humans were the easiest to turn, and once changed, they became immensely loyal to him. He sent them back to spy for him. War councils began drawing this design around their meeting places. Navestrungs could not pass it, and so their plans remained safe.

"As a group, they worked together to create a trap to stop the creature who began all this madness: Devish. Unfortunately, he eluded them. Elexa went after him. She followed his trail, but he sprang a trap that sent her to the heavens. Surprisingly, she found a way to continue to fight from there. From her position, she was able to drive the navestrungs back into the depths of the hills. They were all hunted down and killed over the next several months.

"Then her allies focused on finding a way to return Elexa to them. They succeeded in building a portal to where she now resided in the sky, but she never used it. It was probably too late by then. She sacrificed her life to stop those monsters."

"But when the threat was gone, the shakras began disappearing as well. Humans forgot how they worked and tried infusing themselves with its power by grinding them down and eating them. Those that weren't destroyed became lost. I have searched the world trying to find them, but I know where only one shakra is, and that is in your hand," Damien said, pointing to Saphira.

"How do you know so much?" Saphira asked.

"Because, it was once part of my duty to help defeat those demons. I am continuing that pledge by helping you gain the time you need to learn how to use the shakra to its full advantage. It came to your possession, and I don't think that was by accident. I taught you how to destroy a demon before it has gained possession, but I never learned how to drive them out of the bodies. You must learn that, and only the shakra can teach you. While you are learning, this symbol will protect you. You must learn quickly.

"Once the navestrungs know you have the shakra, they will destroy you if they can. Even though they cannot enter this circle, they can send others who are not possessed to pull you out. I will stop that from happening as long as I can."

"I will do what I can to help, too." Elena placed a hand on Saphira's shoulder.

"But I don't even know how to begin."

"Don't look to me for the answers," Damien said. "Look to the stone. Search within yourself for the answers it can give you. The drawings around you are designed to help you focus and understand the messages of the shakra."

Saphira stood in the center of the room and stared blankly at the shakra in her hand. It shimmered pleasantly, but Saphira wasn't inspired. She thought back to when she was trapped with the navestrung and how she had gotten it to work. She had to focus on the light and what it represented. She decided to try focusing on it again. The light from the stone grew stronger. The room brightened, but it wasn't the right kind of force needed. She took the opposite approach and focused on the darkness behind the light, and the shakra shut down.

She dropped to her knees and looked at the floor instead. Maybe the symbols contained a clue to her next step. The lines were stylized, which made them harder to figure out, but she was almost sure one design represented Reiser who had escaped his beheading by flying away on the back of a bird he had befriended. They had flown so high, he developed blisters on his back and arms. When they popped, the bird's feathers stuck to him, and he later used them to fly around the world. The motif next to it reminded her of Princess Nabell who saved her husband's life by blinding the would-be assassin with a pocket mirror.

She changed the direction of her thoughts. This time she considered the ways light was associated with pain. She imagined sunburns, fires, lightning, and blindness. Beams of light shot out from the shakra. One of them caught the side of Elena's shirt.

"Ow. Don't aim it at me," Elena said, but Saphira just smiled as she looked at her shakra. Maybe she could get this to work after all. She tried to think of other ways light could cause injury when she heard something banging against the wall.

"I think they've discovered where we are," Damien said.

"Already?" Elena asked. "I thought we'd have more time."

"So did I."

The door began to shake, and they could just make out the muffled sound of someone shouting. The shaking and pounding took on a more rhythmic pattern as something hit the door.

"Saphira, what are you doing?" Damien yelled at her when he noticed her watching the door. "Don't ignore the only weapon you have. Activate it again." Saphira tried to concentrate on her "light" weapons again, but she didn't think it would be enough to stop whatever was coming through.

The door began to creak, and the smashing took on renewed vigor. The door finally crumbled, and a big metal pole burst into the room followed closely by dozens of gnomes. A little behind them stood Jack, steeped in rage.

"So, my pretty little flower has a nasty thorn. Why didn't you tell me you had a shakra? That wasn't very kind of you to lie to me, and then destroy the demon. He didn't do anything to you. I was going to let you have a chance for eternal life and riches by my side, but you are full of secrets. Why don't you hand the shakra over to me, and I'll promise not to kill you or your friends."

Jack tried to walk towards Saphira but was repulsed by the symbol on the floor.

"What's this?" He looked down an expression of pure anger on his face. "More tricks and sorcery. If you won't give it to me the easy way, then I'll take it from you the hard way. Guards! Seize her."

At this point, Damien suddenly materialized before the mob. Saphira had been so focused on the door, and then Jack, she hadn't realized he disappeared. The gnomes emitted terrified shrieks as Damien threw walls of fire at them and ripped into them with his claws when they got too close. Some tried to retreat to the hallway, but Jack forced them forward.

"Go back there and fight. No one is leaving until I have the humans and their shakra in my hands. So one dragon has managed to survive? So what? He is not invincible. There is no way he can stop all of you."

The gnomes re-formed and tried to get past Damien. As they advanced, he cut deep holes in their lines. Elena picked up a weapon a gnome had dropped after fighting Damien and began to take on a few gnomes of her own. She had little form, but she energetically attacked them over and over again.

She managed to wound enough of them that they tried to stay away from her swinging arm.

Saphira activated her shakra's deadly powers and directed them towards the advancing gnomes. Red hot beams of light shot out of the stone, causing shirts and pants to burst into flames. Through the smoke, she saw gnomes clawing at their eyes and screaming in frustration before groping around blindly for a way out of the mess around them. But their efforts weren't enough. Gnomes continued to press into the room.

Elena was struggling against the gnomes on her side of the circle when one of them finally managed to knock her sword out of her hand. She still tried to fight them off: punching, scratching, kicking, and biting, but they soon overpowered her and pulled her out of the circle. Saphira saw them taking her over to where Jack stood. An evil smile distorted his lips.

Saphira had enough. How dare Jack do this, and become this evil thing. If killing him would save her friends, then she would do everything she could to stop him. She started to aim the shakra at Jack. As soon as she had a clear shot, she raised her shakra so she could focus on both it and Jack at the same time.

She fused all her hate and energy into the shakra, but when she looked into his face to deliver the killing shot, she realized she couldn't do it. It wasn't Jack that was causing all these horrible things, it was that thing inside him. It was that same evil thing that tried to hurt her in the cell.

Her focus changed, and all her anger went towards the demon. One of those had forced its way into her Jack. Her kind, smart, and slightly cocky Jack. She remembered the Jack who made her laugh and who knew more constellations and myths than anyone else. She knew he had his imperfections, but she knew what they were. She saw clearly the things that were still Jack, and the parts that were the demon. She remembered the light that sliced through the door frame when she had re-entered the gnome dungeons with Elena and Damien. She wished she could slice him in half, removing the demon induced changes and regaining the Jack she had known.

The shakra glowed again. The light began to gather itself together. It formed a long spear of light that aimed itself straight towards Jack's heart. Saphira gasped as it shot towards Jack. "No!" She tried to call it back, but it was too late. It hit him in the center of his chest, and he slumped to the ground. His collapse made everyone stop. Elena stared at him dumbfounded, and the gnomes dropped their hold on her in surprise.

After those few moments of silence, a gnome stepped around Jack's body and ran down the hallway. Being careful not to touch Jack, the others hurried past his crumpled mass and back the way they had come. Soon, the only ones left standing in the room were Elena, Saphira, and Damien.

Elena ran over to Saphira and gave her a hug. "You saved my life. Thank you. I don't know how much longer I would have survived. I'm so sorry about Jack, though. He deserved a better fate."

"I didn't want to kill him." Saphira said, tears falling from her face. "I tried to stop it in the end, but it was too late."

Damien knelt over Jack's still body. "What are you two crying about?" He asked. "He's not dead."

The King's Secret

"He's not dead!" Saphira jumped up and ran towards him.

"Come over and see for yourself," Damien replied as he moved to the side.

Saphira took one of his hands in hers and began stroking his forehead. "Jack? Can you hear me?"

He groaned, and his eyes blinked apart. "What happened?"

Saphira cried in relief. "You're alive!"

"I guess so." Jack looked around. "Where am I?"

"You're in the kingdom of the gnomes," Saphira told him.

Jack tried to sit up. "Ow." He put a hand against his forehead. "I feel like I got hit in the head with a sledge hammer."

"Do you remember anything?" Damien asked.

Jack looked at Damien, who had turned back into a gnome, before turning to tell his story to Saphira. "I remember working in the mines. The guards were harsh and our meals too small for the labor involved. I refused to live like that. I was going to get back to you or die trying." Jack squeezed Saphira's hand tight.

"There were enough of us that I knew with the right level of coordination, we could get away to freedom. I contacted as many people as I could, and they spread the word to the others I couldn't reach. We had to be very careful. If any of us were caught, then it could jeopardize the whole plan.

"The revolt was planned for the next day when one of our rebellion made a mistake. They took several of us away during the night and shoved us into a separate room. They knew we were all involved to some extent, but they didn't know who had been the main organizer.

"One by one, they took us back to their inquisition rooms. I heard other people screaming as various tortures were applied. When it was my turn, all I remember was being whipped before being immobilized on a rack and stretched until my bones popped. They might have done other things, but I lost consciousness. Eventually they stopped and took me back to the room with the others. They dropped me on the floor before finishing their questioning with the rest of the prisoners.

"Eventually I registered where I was and rolled or somehow maneuvered my body against the wall so I could avoid being stepped on. I was near the door when I overheard some of the guards talking. They didn't know why they bothered to keep us alive, since they were just going to kill us all later. There was no value to be gained by interviewing the leaders. We were humans and all troublemakers.

"They discussed other things they disliked about Brackster and what they would change once they were in power. Attacking the mines first, killing all the humans, and then going after Him. Once in control, they would send the gnome armies after the humans outside the mountains. I couldn't let them harm you, but I had no idea how to stop them. I was powerless – broken and trapped in the cell.

"Somebody must have succumbed to the torture because the next day the guards came in and took me away from the rest of the group. They brought me before their king and forced me to bow before him. They didn't know it at the time, but this gave me the perfect opportunity to reveal what I knew to the king.

"After he commended my bravery and skill in organizing, I arranged to speak to him in private, pretending I would reveal how I outsmarted the guards. Instead, I told him about the plot against his life. To reward me, he wanted to set me over his armies.

"I declined, but he waved my rejection aside like he hadn't heard it. He told me to think about it overnight and then tell him my decision in the morning. He had the guards escort me to a cell where I was to think about the alternative if I declined his offer. They shut the door behind me, and he said something I didn't understand.

"It was after he finished talking that I got the impression I wasn't alone. There seemed to be a darkness moving within the blackness. Before I knew it something had surrounded me, pressing its way into my body through my pores. It was the most horrific experience I have ever had." Jack shuddered.

"After that, it's like a bad dream. I returned to Brackster and pledged my loyalty, I met the troops and led their drills against real animals and prisoners, but I was always conscious of a yearning." Jack stroked the side of Saphira's face slowly.

"I remember thinking you had died, and I felt like I had died too, except I was still going on. Suddenly you were alive, and you were with me again. You came in so much more clearly than all the other images. It was the most glorious feeling. When you were around, my senses were sharper, and I realized how much you meant to me."

Jack took his hand back. "Then I did something that pushed you away, I don't remember what. I heard myself using words and saying things to you that were unforgiveable. I remember threatening you with the worst kind of punishment: Life without the ability to control it." Jack turned his face away.

"It suddenly became clear what had happened to me, but I was powerless to stop it from happening to you. The look of horror in your eyes was so strong, I tried again and again to regain control over my own mind and body, but it was impossible. I could do nothing. I couldn't even slow it down." Tears were streaming down his cheeks, when he faced Saphira again. "I don't know how you escaped, but I'm glad that you did. Please forgive me for what I let happen."

Saphira hugged him. This was the Jack she knew and loved. "Of course I forgive you. I know it wasn't you issuing those awful orders."

"Is the demon really gone, now?" Jack asked.

"Yes," Damien responded.

Jack turned to look at him. "Who are you anyway?"

"He's a friend. You can trust him," Saphira said.

"I need you to tell me everything you know about the king," Damien urged. "If he knows how to create navestrungs, then he must be stopped at all costs. Any little details you know could help us find and destroy him."

"I wish I could help you, but I still have a hard time believing this hasn't all been one giant nightmare. If Saphira wasn't here, I wouldn't believe any of it was real. I do know that after I was 'converted,' as the king put it, we met to talk in his room. He said he understood, more completely than I realized how I felt. He said that the steps one takes to achieve greatness for themselves and their people can be heavy indeed. He himself had undergone the change that I had experienced, but I must never tell anyone that. Several of his friends shunned him afterwards, but it had been necessary.

"People he once trusted betrayed him, and others he had never trusted schemed against him. Still, he had helped his people almost achieve greatness once, and he would do so again. With the disappearance of the shakras and the addition of a new trust-worthy supporter, it was time to prepare for the resurrection of his true identity - Devish."

"No!" Damien called out before he could stop himself.

Saphira, Jack, and Elena looked at Damien confused. "He was the one who led the gnomes during the Elexa wars," Damien explained quickly. "He was the first navestrung. His name became so hated that everyone who had carried that name, changed it, and no one dare name their child Devish after that.

"People searched for years trying to find him within the caves, but he was never found. I hoped his death had simply been missed in the chaos and that his body was mistaken for someone else's, but I must have been wrong.

"The question is what will he do now?" Damien began to pace. "Word travels fast. He'll know that at least one shakra still exists, and it is held by one who can wield it. He would never have attempted another merger or revealed his true name if he thought they were still around. We must get him now before he disappears again. The next time he reappears, there might not be a shakra left to destroy him."

"I'm in. I am not going through all this again," Elena said as she stood up. Saphira and Jack joined her.

They left the heart and arrived on the main streets. The chains the girls had worn were still there, so they put them back on. Jack led the way to the palace and the only hidden room he remembered the king showing him.

Across from a giant mural in the artist's hallway, a door swung open as Jack pressed in the flowers on the second rose. It revealed a cozy series of rooms. The dining room looked like it could hold several people around its large round table. There were various games and cards in the cupboard against the wall. It had a smaller alcove that curved back to the left that wasn't immediately visible when you entered. It had a large fireplace with two comfortable armchairs on either side. There were small tables near the chairs to hold whatever books the person might have chosen to take off the massive bookshelves that lined either side of the fireplace. The warm leather added a comforting layer of scent to the scene. Saphira longed to reach out her hand, take a book, and nestle in one of the chairs.

"Come on. There are other rooms to check before we get too comfortable," Damien said. They found a bed chamber and a bathroom. Everything was neat, tidy, and comfortably built.

"This is an entire suite," Damien said after they searched the last room. "He could hide out here in perfect comfort with no one the wiser."

"All it's missing is food," Elena said

"But he wouldn't need that," Damien noted.

"What do you mean?" Jack asked.

"If he is who you say he is, then he doesn't need to eat or drink to exist."

"But I know he eats. I've had several meals with him."

"I'm not saying he can't, just that he doesn't need to."

"But how is that possible?"

"Jack, when you were possessed, you could have lived forever. You didn't need food or water to live."

"So, what do we do now?" Elena asked.

"Can you think of any other place he might go?" Damien asked Jack. "The palace has gotten a lot larger since I was here last. Maybe he hid in another room somewhere. Was there a particular wing of the palace that he favored?"

"I can think of lots of other places he could go, but none where I think he would go. If he wanted to hide, too many other people would know where they are, and if he wanted to run, they are too confined for that."

"Maybe there's a clue here. Let's look around," Elena said.

After another search, they were still out of luck. They examined every scrap of paper, knocked on walls, and pushed or pulled on everything, hoping they would open another hidden passage.

While the others searched the rest of the rooms, Saphira stayed in the den. She glanced through the titles on the bookshelf before grabbing a pile and heading over to the chair to flip through them. The titles included: The History of Weaponry and War, Herbs and Botanical Remedies, Geology of the World, Spirits and Demons, Bed Time Stories for Your Little One, and Proper Care Of your Wings and Tails.

As she was looking through the last book in her pile she heard Jack's frustrated cry. "This is taking too long. Even if we do find a clue at this point, I don't know how useful it is going to be. We'd never catch him."

"We can't give up hope," Damien said. "It's the only thing we have now."

Before Jack could answer, Saphira yelled, "Come quick. I just found something."

"What is it?" Elena asked as they joined her in the den.

"This book. Look at it." She held the book up to show everyone. "At first I thought it was just like the others, but it's not finished." She showed them the last couple of pages, which were blank.

"I think he was actually writing this himself. It's some type of poetry anthology. Some of the titles are pretty interesting." She read them aloud as she flipped through the book. The others moved so they could read over her shoulder with her, "*Longing for Release, The Glory and Honor of War, Protected,* and *Flight of the Angels*. If we were ever going to get a glimpse into his mind, then this would be it."

"We might as well start with flight," Elena said, "since that's what we think he's doing."

"Agreed," Damien replied.

Saphira began reading.

<u>Flight of the Angels.</u>
With angels wings I take to flight
To rise above the mortal's plight.
Farewell to those who hurt too much,
I soon shall be above your touch.

"What do you think that means?" Elena asked.

"I don't know, but it says, 'above your touch.' Maybe he's going up. Can you think of any rooms he might retreat to that are higher than this one?"

"It would be a brilliant move if he did. We always assumed he went deeper so we didn't search the upper stories as thoroughly," Damien said, looking at Jack again.

"He could have," Jack hesitated, "but I never saw him go higher than this level. I wouldn't have any idea how to narrow down which rooms we should search through."

"What if he went outside first? Could he have hidden on top of the mountain?" Elena asked.

"I wouldn't try hiding there myself. Not much grows up there because it's too cold, so he wouldn't have a lot of things to hide behind. But…no one goes up there, and it's usually so foggy, they wouldn't be able to see much if they did."

Saphira shook her head. "But people could still reach him there. And dragons would be sure to see him on one of their trips over the mountain ridge. He couldn't possibly have remained hidden up there all these years."

"That's assuming we would go that way," Damien replied. "The top is so high, we usually fly around it. To be honest, we never thought he'd head that direction since demons feel more comfortable in the earth. There were a few scouts who searched the top of the mountain, but they never reported seeing anything."

"Heading up looks like our best option. Are there any trails we can take that lead to the top?" Jack asked.

"None that I know of. The people we sent had to forge their own pathways. The highest exit from inside the mountains is known as Ala Hoch, and it will only take you halfway."

"What about these?" Elena asked, pointing to the fireplace.

"What about what?"

"The chimneys. The smoke has to go somewhere doesn't it?"

"I hadn't thought about it."

Jack went over and looked at the inside wall of the fireplace. "It'd be a tight fit, but that might work to our advantage. We can lean our backs against one side and press our legs against the other side. We could use the pressure to shimmy our way up. I'll go up a little ways and see if this option would be worth pursuing further. You guys stay here and wait for me."

Jack climbed into the chimney. Extending his arms and legs out for leverage, he began inching his way up the flue. After several minutes, he called down, "I think I see something, but it might just be the light playing tricks. I need to get closer."

A few grunts later Jack called down, "You'll never believe this, but I think I found his route. There are small stepping stones inside the wall of the chimney, and you'll never guess what they look like?"

"What?"

"Wings."

On Angel Wings

" 'With angel's wings I take to flight.' The poem must be more literal than we thought," Saphira said.

"I didn't think he had that much imagination. It's not one of our strong suits," Damien agreed.

"In that case, this would definitely be a good lead to follow. Jack, I'm going up after you," Saphira called from the bottom of the chimney.

"I don't think that's such a great idea. It could be dangerous," Jack shouted down to her.

"I know, but I have the only weapon he's afraid of." She began to wedge herself up the flue. "If he's hiding up there somewhere, then you won't stand a chance without it, and since you don't know how to use it, I'm coming with you."

"And I'm coming too. I've come too far to be left behind now." Elena positioned herself so she could start her climb after Saphira.

"I'll stay behind and guard the entrance in case we're wrong, and he's behind us. It would be too easy to ambush you inside the chimney. May the gods of success be with you," Damien said.

After a few false starts, Damien lifted Elena onto his shoulders and then grew until she reached the wings.

"Thanks Damien," she called down as he morphed back to his original form.

They climbed the steps for hours because they had to keep stopping to catch their breath in the shallow air.

"We're getting close now," Jack called down to the others as a small breeze found his face.

Half an hour later, they crawled out through a small hole onto the top of the mountain. It was bitingly cold. Clouds obscured their vision and frost clung to the ground around them. They rested against the side of a rock until they were ready to start walking again.

They looked back at the entrance and could barely distinguish it from its surroundings. The hole merged seamlessly with the shadow of the shallow overhang. Their footprints would be no help either. They barely made an impression on the hard, barren earth. Saphira ripped some fabric off her dress and tied it around a nearby rock before they began looking around in earnest for any sign of Devish.

They had hoped to find some scraped snow or signs of a recently dislodged rock, but the only changing thing was the wind that constantly blew in their faces. "We had better stick together," Jack said, his nose already bright red. "We don't know where he could be, and he could use his knowledge of the area to ambush us at any time."

They walked around one more time but didn't find anything. At this point, all three were beginning to feel the numbing effects of the cold.

"We should have brought warmer clothes." Saphira rubbed her hands along her arms and blew into her fingers. "I've never been so chilled in my life."

"Let's head back to the chimney. It's at least sheltered from the wind, and we can talk about what we should do next from there," Elena said, her teeth chattering together.

They traveled back to where they thought the entrance to the chimney should be, but they couldn't find it. "Where's our cloth? We tied it right next to the entrance, but I don't see it anywhere," Saphira said as she searched, her voice close to desperation.

They reached under ledges, hoping each small cave would lead them back to shelter, but they were all too shallow.

"What do we do now?" Elena asked.

"I don't know, but if I don't get some heat soon, then I'm going to freeze to death. My body can't take this much longer," Saphira said.

They went over to the nearest overhang where they were partially protected from the bitter wind and huddled together for warmth while they discussed their options.

"Do you think Damien will hear us if we yell to him? He could climb up and let us know where the hole is," Saphira suggested.

"We could try, but it would be too late to save us if it takes him as long as it took us. That was not as easy climb," Jack replied.

"Well, I'm willing to give him the chance to save us." Elena stood up. She walked around the mountain again crying, "Help, Damien. Can you hear us? Help!" The other two quickly followed and began shouting as well. "Damien, we need you. Where are you?"

Elena lost her footing on a slippery rock and stumbled, catching herself on a small boulder. When she moved her hand away, some snow came off – revealing a small set of scratches in the rock. "Saphira, Jack," she called, "look at this."

When they arrived, Elena looked at Saphira and asked, "Saphira, do you remember when you had a vision of the northern cave?"

Jack turned towards Saphira. "Vision?"

"I'll tell you about it later," Saphira promised.

Elena continued, "Do you happen to remember what the edges looked like?"

"Yes. There were deep gouges everywhere, like something with sharp claws had used it as a launching pad."

"And remember how you said there was something odd about the entrance. Now, look at this rock's lip."

Saphira put her hand against the edge and ran her fingers over it. "It's scratched. So what?"

"That's what I thought at first, but what would scratch it up here? Then I remembered the cave. These marks match it exactly. I think it might be a form of writing."

They wiped off as much as the remaining snow as they could and leaned in, trying to get a better look.

"You two are crazy," Jack said. "There's no way we'll be able to decipher it. All we need to know is that it does not mark our entrance back to safety. Those runes could mean anything. This symbol right here," he said pointing to one of the symbols, "looks like a block version of Elexa's constellation, but it could mean death to all cats. We are wasting our time, and should go back to trying to find the chimney."

Saphira ignored the last part of his tirade. "Jack, your right. It does look like Elexa. And the one after it could be Tournus, the journey god. Maybe this is some sort of plaque that commemorates the spot where Elexa left for the heavens."

"Maybe, but what if it's more than that? What if this is the portal Damien said they built to get her back down? Do you think it could still be activated? The poem said Devish would be 'above us all.' The heavens are 'above us all.' The wings were literal - his assent could be literal as well. And if Devish figured out a way to make it work, then we can too," Elena said.

The girls turned to the writing with renewed interest. "Girls!" Jack called, but they ignored him. They stared at the stone, rubbing their fingers along the writing to see if they could interpret it, or if it could be pushed in to reveal a secret chamber.

A particularly cold wind blew by, and Saphira leaned in closer to the rock to avoid it. Suddenly the runes started to glow. Both Jack and Elena stared at her. "Saphira what did you do?"

"Nothing." Saphira straightened her back, and the runes returned to their normal color.

"Did you see that?" Elena asked Jack.

"Yes, lean in again."

She did, and the symbols started to glow, starting from Saphira's center point.

"Saphira, where is your shakra?" Jack asked.

Saphira blushed. "It's in here." Saphira pointed to her bodice. "It was easier to keep it in there while we were climbing than to hold it in my hands. I'll get it out." She turned her back to the others and pulled out the shakra. She held it out and ran it across the runes. They all lit up this time. Their light came together and fused to become one big disc. It then expanded out until it made a circular frame, large enough for a person to fit through.

"Well, I think we found our portal," Elena said, and they went through one by one. They stepped into a world unlike anything they had ever known before. The land was wrapped in a blue fog. The stars were still above them, but they were much bigger than before. Below them, the ground was clear. They saw where they had been standing seconds ago, but it was thousands of feet below them now. As they stared, the ground below seemed to rise up to meet them. When they glanced away, it went back to the size it had been before.

"We're here but I wish I knew where here was," Saphira said, looking at her new surroundings.

"It's Ambrosia, the starlings' kingdom. I'm so sorry you won't be around to enjoy this view much longer," a voice said from behind them. Elena whirled around just in time to see Saphira crumble to the ground. Her attacker smiled at Elena before he hit the side of her head with the butt of his sword. She fell down next to Saphira as Jack drew his sword and waved it at Devish.

Land Of The Starlings

"Stop right there. Your time has come, and I'm going to bring you to justice," Jack challenged Devish.

"Interesting words for someone whose life I saved. I thought you were bringing them to me, but it appears I was mistaken." Devish tightened his grip on his sword. "There's something different about you, but what?"

"I no longer have your evil symbiote living in my body. That is what's different."

"Impossible."

"No, it's not impossible."

"What I mean is – I'm sorry. I had no idea the relationship with your enhancer was so bad that you considered it evil."

"You mean the demon you trapped inside my body?" Jack swung his sword at Devish, who stayed out of reach.

"No, I mean the old soul I merged with your body to benefit both of you. That is how it is supposed to be. I offered you something no mortal could ever hope to achieve. I offered you a chance to have eternal life. Not just for yourself, but for anyone else you wanted to give it to. You would be able to experience eternal love. Who else can make that claim and really mean it. Just imagine what you two could have accomplished together," Devish reasoned as he and Jack circled each other.

"Surely you must long for something great and noble. I gave you the time to actually do it. What can any one man do in the lifetime assigned to him by nature? Nothing! Everything he creates goes away after his death – his vision distorted and abused until it has been completely destroyed by those whom he foolishly entrusted with his work. Do you want that to happen to you? Do you want everything you stood for and built up to crumble to dust? Don't you want what you do to matter?"

"Nice try, but I'm not going to fall for it. I experienced your 'salvation,' and I know what it means. There's no room for love with that being of hate filling your body. You can do nothing to fight it. That is not saving or helping people. It destroys them. I would rather have a short life, filled with the potential for love and peace, than an eternity with such rage and suspicion."

"You don't understand. I'm not offering you that. Do I look like I'm filled with murderous hate?" Devish lowered his point to the ground. "I saved your life, and I could have killed your friends just now, but I didn't. I realize, now, that I made a mistake. I didn't prepare you correctly. I thought I had, because you became joined, but I was wrong. You must have fought it. It must have sensed your struggle and resented you for it. If you had just let it enter, then it would have shared your mind more harmoniously and there wouldn't have been any struggle for dominance. There would be no hate.

"If you work together, if you embrace its presence, then it nourishes you completely, body and soul. Those first few moments can be critical in the bonding process and how your relationship is going to work. We can try again, and this time we will do it right, and you will see the harmony that I am talking about." Devish extended his free hand towards Jack.

Jack jerked away. "Never!"

Devish raised his sword. "You're making a big mistake. Think about what one jointure has already accomplished. Under my leadership, the gnome kingdom is strong again. We are getting the respect that has been denied us for so long. People used to dismiss us as being just another creature, at best. At worst, we were their nightmares: the epitome of every human weakness and fault. We were vain, greedy, stupid, ambitious, deceitful, and untrustworthy.

"'What have the gnomes ever done?' they asked. 'What noble thing have they accomplished?' But they aren't asking those questions now, are they? No. We are strong. No one questions what we can do anymore. Would you take that away from us? Would you have us go back to being treated like scum?"

"It's not respect they're showing, it's fear."

Devish snarled in response, "You lie! Your people bow before me and trade on *my* terms. Those are tokens of respect that are universally recognized. You don't bow down to people you view as weak and stupid."

"But you force them to bow down. Real respect comes when people bow when they don't have to. You can force people to do many things, but just because they obey, it doesn't mean they honor you or won't betray you the first chance they get."

Devish struggled to gain control over his emotions. "You are young and inexperienced. Don't you think I've been around long enough to see how things really work? You are still idealistic and don't understand that obedience is the first part of respect. Over time, people will realize how much better they are under my rule; then we will earn their private regard as well. Obedience is better than nothing.

"They might not do it willingly at first, but humans are naturally resistant to change. They cannot see how things could be better. That takes true vision. After the new order is in place, they will begin to understand and acceptance will come. You knew that for a time."

"That was when my mind was clouded and disturbed. Now that I am liberated I see things the way they are again. It is that demon inside you that is giving you false ideas. You should reject him so you can view the world without its blinding filter on and become a real asset to your people." Jack released a hand from his sword and held it out towards Devish. "Put down your sword so we can help you."

"Don't be a fool," Devish said, and Jack brought his hand back to his sword's hilt. "You say my mind has been clouded by the demon, but yours has been impaired by the shakra. It has hurt your judgment more certainly than anything else. Throw your shakra towards me, and we can discuss our options reasonably."

###

Saphira's head was aching, and she shut her eyes again almost as soon as she opened them. She knew she was face down, and Elena lay next to her. The ground felt soft, like grass after a rainstorm. She heard two people fighting in the background but didn't care who they were. She placed her arms under her shoulders and prepared to sit up.

Looking through one eye at a time, she pushed her upper body off the ground. Between her hands stood the peak they had been on just a few seconds before. The ground rose towards her until she could distinguish figures coming out of the mountains. She looked closer and realized they were gnomes. Thousands of them were marching out of the tunnels. There were more tunnels in those mountains than she thought anyone was aware of. The land seemed to be hemorrhaging gnomes. This was no flight, however.

Each gnome carried a sword, spear, or crossbow and moved with the determination and rhythm of a war party. She could see the glint of the sun off their blades and armor as they marched to the first town. She watched as they moved around the buildings. Houses were set ablaze, and the only ones who left the buildings were the ones who went in.

Saphira glanced down the trail they were taking and didn't see any forces gathering that would be able to stop their progress. If they kept the same course and speed, then they would reach King Cedric' castle in less than twenty-four hours. The king would be captured, and without leadership, they wouldn't stand a chance.

"No!" The sound involuntarily escaped her lips. Jack, surprised at her voice, turned to face her. When Jack's head turned towards Saphira, Devish attacked. Catching Jack off guard he was able to wound him in the stomach, but with the instinct of self-preservation, Jack moved away before the sword could pierce any vital organs.

"What is it?" Jack asked her as he fended off the king's attacks.

"The army. The gnomes. They're attacking," Saphira said.

"So this was all just a ploy to buy time for your armies," Jack accused Devish.

"No. They had standing orders to attack if we should ever be invaded. When your little dragon friend caused all that uproar, the final orders were released, and the armies were set out. Of course I wish you would join me again, but if you won't, then I can't let you live to oppose me." Devish fought Jack again with renewed energy.

"Saphira, quickly use the shakra," Jack called out as he blocked Devish's attacks.

"So it's Saphira who has the shakra. I should have guessed." Devish adjusted his attack so every thrust and parry brought him closer to the girls.

Saphira's head still throbbed, but she found the shakra lying next to her and placed it between her hands. She looked at the stone and tried to focus on the king. She thought of his wars against the other races and believed the world would be better without this delusional creature in it. She put all her might into conjuring up light's offensive moves: splitting things in half, fire, blindness, burns. The shakra pulsated and sent out ray after ray of light, but it wasn't affecting him.

"It's not working," she shouted.

"It must be the demon protecting him," Jack said between breaths. "You've got to try something else. How do you get rid of it?"

Saphira remembered back to the cell. She had focused on positive things, things that were the antithesis of what she was facing. She tried to do this again, and a soft orb came out and surrounded Devish, but he fought Jack with the same stamina and energy as before.

Jack parried a particularly powerful blow that shoved him back several inches and gasped back to Saphira. "Try again. What did you do to free me?"

Saphira focused on the king again, and this time she searched to find the man he might once have been. She wondered what would make him turn to the demons and accept their foul deal. She tried to think of the sadness he must have felt for the plight of his people and his inability to create the world he longed for. She remembered the sacrifice he made and the lives of friends and family that had gone before him. She knew the fear that people felt around him and realized his own lonely state. He was trapped, and though he had initially sought it, he was now caught and could not escape its net. Her shakra started to glow and formed a shaft that pierced him in the heart. Devish fell forward with the weight of the impact. He lay still for several minutes, and Jack leaned in closer to check on him.

When Jack was only a few inches away, Devish opened his eyes and laughed. Blue flames licked merrily behind his eyes. Devish turned his head to look at Saphira. "Is that the best you've got, little girl? Did you really think that you would be able to defeat me and take away the source of my greatness? Did you think I would be as easy as the other ones? You were wrong. I saw how the others fell, and I created protections against those attacks. I am stronger than you can possibly imagine. You cannot kill me, and it's only a matter of time before I destroy you."

With those last words he leapt to his feet and sprang after Saphira. Jack grabbed his legs, and they both fell down. As they struggled, Saphira realized that it was true. The others were forced into unions with the navestrung. Their own spirits had worked with the power of the shakra to push the demons out. Devish, however, didn't want it to happen. He was holding fast onto his immortality and all it offered him, regardless of the consequences. He was not going to give it up, even though it had cost him so much.

She looked back at the stone, and a new idea entered her head. She directed this beam of light at Devish who had escaped Jack and was now racing towards her. Once more, he was hit, but instead of bouncing off, or passing through, it stayed around him. It solidified into a solid, hard sphere of light.

Devish collided with the glowing wall, but to his surprise, he didn't go through. He pounded the edges of the wall, looking for a weakness. "What's this?" he sneered at Saphira. "Another pitiful attempt to overpower me? It won't work. I already told you, you can't kill me."

"I don't intend to. As much as you want to kill us, we don't share your bloodlust. We are only fighting you because of the threat you pose. But if we can take away your power to harm, then we do not need your death to satisfy us. This orb will keep you safe inside its borders where you cannot harm anyone else. I hope you like it, because you'll be in there a long time."

"Do you think you'll be able to stop what's happening by trapping me here? There are others who share my vision and will pick up where I left off. They will destroy you, and when I get out of here, I will return to lead my people."

Saphira turned her attention to Jack. He was bleeding from his wound on the side, but it didn't look too dangerous. She made him take his shirt off and then tied it so the knot was on the opposite side of his waist. She then helped him back into his jacket.

They went back to the portal and turned Elena over. They were relieved when she groaned and asked groggily, "What happened?"

"You were hit over the head, but don't worry, everything is going to be all right now. We found Devish. Jack was able to fend him off until I trapped him in a light prison. He won't be harming anyone again for a very long time."

They helped Elena get up and all three of them headed towards the shimmering outline of the portal. Suddenly, Saphira let out a cry and crumpled to the ground. The shakra rolled out of her hands and blood oozed out of a fresh wound in her back.

"No!" Jack raised his sword as he swirled to face the attacker. Devish was swinging his bright red sword tip through the air, and it collided against Jack's with a clang. Jack kicked him back. "How did you get out?"

"Fool. Did you think you were the only one with a shakra? Didn't you hear me say that you needed one to get up here? There's only one way to save her now, and that's by pairing her up with one who can repair her body. Deny her that, and she dies. Would you have her death on your head?"

"She wouldn't want that kind of life. Her body would live, but she would be gone." Jack savagely lashed out at Devish with his sword, but Devish jumped out of the way.

"No, she wouldn't. With the navestrung's help, a part of Saphira would always be alive."

"Enough. I won't hear any more of your lies." Jack attacked again, using killing strokes with every swing, but Devish had several centuries to perfect his art. Every time Jack attacked, Devish was able to successfully evade his thrusts. Devish was toying with him and laughed after every failed attempt. Jack tried to swing harder, but his wound was finally catching up to him. As the sweat trickled down his forehead, Devish became harder and harder to see.

Jack knew he wouldn't last much longer. He had to find a way to end this. He saw Devish shift his weight to the left, and Jack lifted his sword to attack from the right. Jack heard a low thunk and Devish's eyes grew wide before he collapsed in a heap at Jack's feet. Jack's sword just missed him as it slid through the air and lodged into the ground next to him.

Jack quickly scanned the horizon and saw Elena walking towards him. She carefully walked towards Devish and began feeling the area around his body. She picked up the shakra and handed it to Jack with a shrug. "It's the only thing I could find. I figured if I can knock a squirrel out of a tree, then I can hit him on the head."

Elena began searching his pockets. "We need to hurry and get his shakra from him before he wakes up."

Jack joined her, and they soon found it hanging from a chain around his neck. It was shaped more like a lima bean than an orb, but it had the same translucent quality to it. Jack quickly removed it and handed it to Elena who wrapped it around her own neck.

"What do you want to do now? Should we just leave him here or try one last time to trap him in the light?" Elena asked.

"I wouldn't know how. That was something Saphira did. Do you know how to work the shakra?"

Elena shook her head. "No. When Damien was trying to help Saphira destroy the demon in her cell, he mentioned focusing on positive things like light, joy, and goodness. But Damien said there is a different process to destroy demons that have joined with a body. Saphira never mentioned how she saved you. There wasn't time."

Jack looked at the shakra in his hands. "I wish I knew how to activate this so I could help him the way I was helped. No matter what he hoped he would gain, he must know by now that it was not worth it. I think it has just been too long. He hardly remembers who he is anymore, the way he was before the demon joined him."

"Yes, but you know exactly what demons are, and what they are like. You could probably guess better than anyone what he could have been like. Who he is inside that mess. Would it be worth it to take him down and have Saphira try to save him when she recovers, or should we just kill him now while he's unconscious? Even a navestrung couldn't survive having its head cut off...right?"

Jack looked at Devish and pictured the demon. He remembered its hunger, its greed, and its power. He tried to remember everything that defined it. He then thought about everything he knew about Devish and tried to separate the two. He remembered conversations they had and impulses he had felt coming from Devish. There were two beings intertwined before him: The demon and the imperfect gnome, and he knew them both. Alike in their desire for greatness, they only differed in the lengths they were willing to go to achieve that greatness. Devish was willing to sacrifice himself, but he wouldn't have sacrificed his people.

The stone was glowing, but Jack barely noticed it. The light interlaced like a net as it spread itself over Devish's body and disappeared into his skin. Jack took a step back.

"What did you do?" Elena asked when the light faded.

"I don't know. I was trying to discover who Devish really was. Just when I thought I figured it out, he was covered with light."

"Whatever you did, we won't know its effect until he wakes up." She looked up at him. "Is that something we want to happen?"

Jack's eyebrows knit together. "Yes," he paused, "I think it is."

"Then we'll keep him for Saphira. I'll tend to her wounds and try to get her stabilized so we can get her to a doctor. You stay close to him so that if he wakes up and tries to attack us again, you can stop him."

Elena took Jack's coat and ripped it up. She created a cloth pad and placed it directly over the wound. She then knotted strips of fabric together so they could secure the pad to Saphira's back. "I think this should slow the bleeding, but she doesn't look good. Her breathing is shallow, and she's not responding to what I'm saying. We need to get her in the hands of a professional soon."

Jack leaned over Devish's body and checked his pulse. "He's still alive, but either you hit his head's weak spot, or the shakra did something to really shake him up, because he doesn't look like he's going to wake up very soon. I'll take Saphira through the portal if you think you can handle him."

"As long as he's content to be dragged."

"I don't think he'll object. Let's get out of here."

Jack picked Saphira up as smoothly as he could, careful not to disturb her bandages. Elena wasn't nearly as gentle. She propped Devish up just enough to get her arms under his shoulders and began dragging him backwards toward the portal home. Just before she passed through, she thought she saw something in the fog. It looked like a human raising its hand in a farewell gesture, but it couldn't be. Just when she was sure it was, the portal lit around her, and she was back on the mountain.

The Last Reunion

The wind had not lessened while they were gone. If anything, then it had increased. Elena shivered. "I forgot about this weather." She turned around to face Jack and Saphira. "She can't survive like this for long, and we still have no idea where the entrance to the chimney is. Do you think Damien heard us earlier and will be able to find us?"

"Was there ever any doubt?" Damien asked from somewhere above them.

"Damien!" They shouted as he landed gently beside them.

"What happened to Saphira?" he asked, nuzzling her arm.

"Sword wound to the back. We'll explain what happened later. Right now, we have to get her to a doctor," Elena told him.

"Done." Damien yelled, "Sondra," and a yellow dragon swooped down from the sky to join them. Elena and Jack both took a step back. "The girl, Saphira, needs your help. Take her back to my cave and treat her."

"I'll make her as good as new in no time." Sondra pinched her claws together as she moved her paw to the side, making an oval. A cloud appeared and Sondra said, "Just put her down there, Sugar." Jack placed her gently on the floating cushion after making sure it would hold her weight.

Elena stared at Sondra. Her voice was so familiar, but she didn't know why. Before she could figure it out, Sondra had flown away, blowing the cot gently in front of her.

"Now let's see who else you managed to wound up there?"

Elena dropped her charge and moved out of the way so he could see better.

"Devish! I guess I should have known you would be the ones to defeat him. My other friends will be so disappointed." Elena and Jack looked up in the sky and saw four other dragons flying around. "I had promised them action, but it looks like all they'll be now are carriers."

"But there are still several gnomes on the move. They were heading towards our castle," Jack said. He started to run to the side of the mountain where the fighting was, but winced in pain.

Damien raised a claw, stopping Jack as his eyes scanned his body. "Your wounds are simple enough we can treat them right here."

"Don't worry about me, help my people." Jack tried to wave him off.

"I'm afraid there's not much need for our presence there. We were going to have a thunderous reintroduction to the humans as we drove the gnomes from their castle walls at the last minute, but our entrance got spoiled. The humans were waiting for them in the woods outside the castle and ambushed them. So you see, we really do have time for you."

Damien began to hum softly to himself while four other dragons landed. A yellow mist formed around Jack. He tried to back away, but it pressed in closer until it penetrated his skin. His scream turned into a sigh of relief. He removed his shirt and stared at where the wound once was. His skin was perfectly smooth now.

Meanwhile, one of the two red dragons shuffled over to Elena's passenger and hissed when the face came into view. Damien twisted his head towards Elena. "Tell me. How did you defeat him?"

Elena looked at Jack before asking, "Is he really defeated, or will he come back?"

Damien studied Devish. "He is not dead, but he is not going to wake up anytime soon, I can promise you that. There is something else as well, but we will have to wait until he wakes up until I can be sure what it means." Damien turned to the other red dragon. "Chrisper, take Devish to the place we discussed for him." Chrisper nodded and scooped him up in his claws. As he flew away, Devish's feet knocked against one of the boulders so hard, his shoe fell off.

"Chrisper." Damien warned, and Chrisper flew higher.

Damien turned back to Jack and Elena. "It seems like the biggest threats have already been handled. It's not as prestigious, but do you want to join our hunt for stragglers?"

Elena said, "No," at the exact same moment Jack said, "Yes."

"I've had enough excitement for one day," Elena explained. "Jack, since you actually got the shakra to do something for you, why don't you take it and help Damien and his friends finish unearthing the enemy? I'd like to be there for Saphira when she wakes up." She looked at Damien who nodded. She then handed Jack Saphira's shakra.

"Oh, I almost forgot. This is one, too." Elena removed the chain from her neck, and when the second shakra hit the light, Damien's teeth snapped together so forcefully, the sound echoed down the mountain.

"Where did you find that? That's one of ours."

"Devish," Jack replied and Damien spit out a flame of fire so large, the other dragons backed away. Damien spoke quickly. "Enil, take Elena back to my cave, and the rest of you come with me. I've got some deaths to deliver."

Devish woke up to a giant eye guarding his cell. He didn't say anything. He just lay there and looked at it. The dragons confirmed that he was still a navestrung, but Jack had somehow managed to contain the demon. It no longer had control of Devish's body. Most of who Devish was had disintegrated over time, and now the navestrung was trapped the way Devish had been, although it didn't look like it would have to suffer as long as Devish did. He was dying. His body was breaking down, and there was nothing anyone could do to stop it. Not that they tried.

Saphira's recovery was intentionally slow because the nerves could not be aided in their recovery by magic without suffering some damage. She made steady progress, and after a few days, she was allowed to walk short distances around the room. At Elena's request, Damien brought the girls some new dresses, and Jack visited as often as he could, but he was kept busy negotiating a truce between the parties.

Jack had a difficult time finding someone who could represent the gnomes in the treaty process. Their king was incapacitated, Jack was rejected, and their other leaders were either dead or in hiding. To make matters even more complicated, a movement was growing among the gnomes to choose a king from the old line, a descendent of King Hagan. King Hagan had ruled over one of the most peaceful times in their history and was regarded as one of their greatest kings.

However, the lineage would be hard to prove since the heir had gone into hiding after Devish's hostile takeover. He never came back after Devish was defeated, and it was assumed he died before he could assume his true identity again. His descendants, if he had any, might not even know they were royalty. Supporters of the Hagan plan found an old tapestry of the family and decided to match everybody up against the last known likenesses. Whoever most closely resembled the family would get their support.

The gnome they finally chose as their king did not even know about the event until the day it was happening. He was just exiting from a tunnel that led to one of the deep mines when a group found him and dragged him along with them. When he entered the hall, he walked straight towards the tapestry. Tears filled his eyes, and he caressed the fabric gently with his hands. As he stood there, whispers began to fill the hall as others noticed how closely he resembled the lost heir, Damien. They asked him his name, and when it matched the lost king's, doubters became believers and their support tripled. Damien was elected the new ruler and crowned with a great deal of ceremony.

Jack was surprised he recognized the new king when he came in to finalize the gnomes' part of the treaty. Any fear he had about the new ruler's attitude towards humans went away, and they were able to reach an agreement everyone could accept.

Saphira and Elena smiled when they heard. They thought Damien would make a great ruler, but they wondered how the gnomes would react if they ever found out they elected a dragon. As part of the treaty, all the humans working for the gnomes were freed, and Elena was reunited with her family. She still spent a lot of time with Saphira however, and when Saphira asked her about it, she explained that she no longer felt as comfortable with them. "They look at me oddly sometimes, like they don't know or trust who I am anymore."

When Saphira finally heard one of the stories that had sprung up about them, she was no longer surprised at their reaction. Elena was being hailed as a hero, while she and Jack were called mages for their control of the shakra. To hear them tell it, Elena sliced off the heads of 30 gnome combatants while she and Jack vaporized a hundred more, each, before the fighting was over. She didn't know how anyone could take them seriously.

She was laughing over the latest exaggeration with Elena when a young soldier found them. He thumped his fist against his chest and bowed deeply before them. When he rose, he said, "Your Greatnesses, it's an honor to finally make your acquaintance. I am sorry to greet you in this garb, but I have just come from the gnome tunnels where we have successfully cleared the last chamber of rebels. As the royal representative, I came here to thank the ladies who bravely faced and defeated the navestrungs, making my job possible. I wanted you to know how deeply your prince stands in your debt."

He took off his helmet and Elena exclaimed, "But we know you! You're not the prince, you're a guard."

Jillian looked confused. "I am the prince, but no one was supposed to know I double as a guard. The uniform and rules were designed to make it impossible for strangers to recognize me."

"But we aren't strangers. At least Stephen and Peter weren't. Why didn't you tell us…them, you were something more?" Elena asked, her eyebrows knotted together.

"Stephen and Peter? Where are they?" He looked around the room quickly. "I'm sorry, but I've been worried about them. No one else has heard anything about them. Are they all right?"

"Yes, they are fine," Saphira said.

"Do you know where I can find them? I would love to hear what happened to them after we separated."

He looked from one girl to the next. The girls were holding a silent conversation. Elena's fingers began to tap and he recognized the ring on her finger.

His mouth dropped open. "You're not?" He looked at them closer. "Are you, *them*?" Saphira nodded, laughing inside at his level of shock. Jillian stepped back. "Why didn't you tell me? I would never have let you come here alone, if I had known."

Elena covered her ring with her other hand. "I hope you're not too disappointed."

"Disappointed? How could I be? It would just appear that I am even more indebted to you than I realized. I admit I had my suspicions, but I couldn't convince myself that girls would do everything you two did. Obviously I was wrong. I hope *you're* not disappointed to find out that I'm the prince."

"Of course we're not. Why would we be?" Elena asked.

"Because of my father. He was not as good to you as he should have been."

"But you made up for it by your own behavior towards us and your country. We heard that you were able to get your army together in time to stop the first attack." Saphira said.

"Yes. After you left, I went to the town leaders and begged them to give me as many men as they could spare. I told them everything I had heard, and what I thought it added up to, but they were still hesitant. I wished I could have spoken with your feeling," Jillian said, looking at Elena.

"Ultimately, I convinced them to let me take the men to a special training camp where we would practice war drills with techniques that have proven to be the most successful against the gnomes. I promised the leaders of the towns that the men could return when the camp was over.

"I sent groups of them to visit all the nearby cities and gather as many men as they could. I warned them to keep it quiet so the gnomes wouldn't know we suspected anything, or be able to guess how many men we were training to fight. At first our numbers were small, but more men started to join us after rumors spread about gnomes attacking some bordering farms and villages, torturing people for information.

"We divided into battalions, and I had the men practice fighting along the slopes and hitting targets from many different angles and distances. We had just finished training when someone ran into our camp screaming that the gnomes were coming. We kept our camp together, knowing we were in the best place to fight them and waited for them to come to us. Some of the men were frightened now that their practice was now a reality, but they took courage from their companions and fought well."

Jillian looked down and shook his head. "I don't want to think what might have happened if we hadn't been ready." He looked up. "If it hadn't been for you, I might have waited too long to act. Without the discipline and trust they had in our training and each other, they would have fled with the first wave of attack. The king's city would have been overrun, my father captured, and no one prepared to stop them from spreading their carnage. I honor you. Both of you," he said, turning to include Saphira back into the conversation, "and I want you to know that if there is anything I can do for you or your families, you have but to ask."

"Thank you, but that is not why we did what we did," Elena replied.

"I know, and that is what makes your actions so noble. I do hope you will consider the castle your home until new ones can be built for you, and afterwards, too. You would be welcome to stay for as long as you wanted."

Jillian stopped talking and Saphira glanced at Elena who stared back at him with a soft smile on her face. They seemed to have forgotten her, because when she said, "Of course we will," they both startled.

Jillian recovered first. "I will send someone to make the arrangements now. As soon as you are ready to leave, I will personally escort you there." He smiled as he added, "Using the main roads this time."

As soon as he was gone, Saphira gently nudged her friend and said, "It sounds like someone has a romantic rendezvous planned."

Elena swatted her arm away. "I don't know what you're talking about. I'm sure he would have extended that same offer to anyone. He was just being courteous."

"Oh, I don't deny he has good manners, but I noticed that he had a hard time taking his eyes off you. And he definitely drew closer to you than he did to me while we were traveling together."

"You are just imagining things," Elena said, but her gaze drifted back to the door Jillian had exited through.

Saphira followed her gaze and said, "I don't think so, and I don't think you do either. Once you admit it, I'll be the happiest person in the world."

Elena blushed. "You're being ridiculous."

"No I'm not," Saphira grinned at her friend. "I'm being insightful. And wasn't I supposed to help you find your true love, anyway? I think I remember you saying something like that after Jack left...."

Printed in Great Britain
by Amazon.co.uk, Ltd.,
Marston Gate.